The Brainstorm

The Brainstorm

Jenny Turner

JONATHAN CAPE
LONDON

Published by Jonathan Cape 2007

2 4 6 8 10 9 7 5 3

First published in Great Britain in 2007 by
Jonathan Cape
Random House, 20 Vauxhall Bridge Road,
London SW1V 2SA

www.randomhouse.co.uk

Addresses for companies within The Random House Group Limited
can be found at:
www.randomhouse.co.uk/offices.htm

The Random House Group Limited Reg. No. 954009

A CIP catalogue record for this book
is available from the British Library

ISBN 9780224078047

The Random House Group Limited makes every effort to ensure that the
papers used in its books are made from trees that have been legally sourced
from well-managed and credibly certified forests. Our paper procurement
policy can be found at: www.randomhouse.co.uk/paper.htm

Printed and bound in Great Britain by
Mackays of Chatham plc
Chatham, Kent

For the catastrophe will have to have been of such a kind that it was not and has not been – except perhaps by a very few – recognised as a catastrophe. We shall have to look not for a few brief striking events whose character is incontestably clear, but for a much longer, more complex and less easily identified process and probably one which by its very nature is open to rival interpretation.

Alasdair Macintyre

Hope, hope, hope, little bunnies, hope hope hope.

James Kelman

In memory of my brother, Roderick Turner (1965–2001)

Chapter One

Lorna looked around her, puzzled. Good, she thought, I'm still here then. I'm sitting in an office. I have a desk and chair.

She was sitting at a curved grey workstation, in front of a large and ugly computer. The computer had an email open, screeds and screeds of typed words. To her left, a blonde girl was riffling angrily through a ring binder. Her desk was much the same as Lorna's, only neater, with a tall vase of orange lilies rising to the roof. To her right, a window told her she was sitting high up in a modern tower, looking down on a stretch of motorway, with high flats and slabs of golden council housing. The sky behind was dark blue, bristling with ions. The computer screen in front of her was just as deep, just as gorgeous, just as forbiddingly charged.

'You are your own worst enemy,' said the email. It then proceeded to go on and on.

'You're a fucking nightmare, a total fucking nightmare,' the email continued, immobile and unshiftable on the frozen screen.

She had been tired, she remembered, with an infinite dryness. Her head clanged with noise and agitation. Hot fronts and cold fronts sloshed around the sky. There had been pressure, and a flickering, and a failure. 'Thief. Bully. Hypocrite,' said the email. 'I am sick of you and your butter wouldn't melt.'

Lorna pushed a button once and the whole screen blackened. She pushed the button a second time. The computer, radiantly free of scolding emails, glowed and sighed back to life.

Lorna stole a look at her next-door colleague, an operation that, she discovered, was not so easy to do. Someone had erected a barricade of plastic letter trays and magazine holders, caulked with padded envelopes and old newspapers, on top of the side-desk extension in between. But Lorna could see that the girl was working furiously, and that her forehead was dry and tense. Her hair was also dry-looking, so smooth and flat you could see the scissor-marks, and the added highlights in thin stripes.

So, can I trust her? Lorna silently asked the secret self we all have deep inside ourselves, if only things are quiet enough around it to let it be heard. Her secret self responded with another question. Why then did you bother erecting this barricade?

Lorna turned her chair to look behind her, letting her eye sweep around the office floor. It was huge, like a park, but low-ceilinged, with walls of glass. It was crammed with workstations, broken up by banks of shelves. An executive cubicle jutted out at the far corner, with glass walls and potted-plant screening and beautiful flush doors. On the partition wall opposite, a sign had the name of a famous newspaper on it, etched in black on a sheet of thinnest tin. The same newspaper was heaped up in piles underneath it, and in more piles by the window, and in a smaller pile on Lorna's desk. I'm in the office of a famous newspaper, she decided. The question was whether she was meant to be, and if she was, in what way. Just trying to frame the question made her feel alarmed and shaky. Her eye fell on a packet of cigarettes and a lighter. A passageway through the problem seemed to open up.

In her head, Lorna saw herself push her chair out, rise from her desk and walk, in a usual-looking manner, round the side of the partition to where the ladies' toilet was bound to be. The phone went; she picked it up without thinking. Hello?

Hello, said a man's voice; I'm looking for Lorna.

2

I'll see if I can find her for you, she said politely, and put the phone straight down.

She shrugged her bottom to check that the chair was on a swivel and peeped down briefly into the darkness underneath. She was pleased to see that she had shiny boots on, little ankle boots with a dinky heel. The thought that the boots pleased her came disconnected, in a balloon, and when she grasped to see where it had come from, off it went. She did not know why the boots were a good sign. Apparently they were, though. Fine.

London was more fun on the whole then, back in the mid-to-late 1990s. You could feel the wealth, the energy, the envy build up in places, causing pressure. You could see it almost, jumping and sparking, from one tall building to the next. The city looked like a graph sometimes, a great histogram of bouncing value. Tiny men in hard hats and yellow jerkins struggled against the horizon with their cranes and diggers. Hanks of fibre-optic cable were sunk in ditches under ground.

Lorna could not really tell this from the window, but the building she was in was famous for its bulk, and its opulent brushed-steel cladding, and for the deeply scary speed with which it had gone up in the first place, only to stand there empty for ages until the rents were dropped. It was squarish in conception, tall but also squat, and was pointed at the top, like a blunted pencil. From its tenth floor downwards, it spread out on a wide, curved horizontal, like a space fort or a giant hovercraft, with hundreds of tiny windows. Prestige developments of that period were often shaped to look like toys of one sort or another, over-dressed in glass and steel and marble. It was an affectation, and thus an example of function dictating form.

The building perched, with its heavy brethren, on a spur of artificial land reclaimed from the surrounding water. Its foundations were laid on piles and coffer dams, hundreds of metres deep. The glittering castellations touched actual ground only glancingly. The entire edifice was held up for the most part on an elaborate system of cross-loaded decks. A curvy bridge joined the new land to the old world on the other side of the bit of water. A rag of hazard tape marked the spot under the northeast portico where a maintenance worker had been killed the other week when a sheet of glass sheared off.

Security guards, in their yellow high-vis jerkins, were hired to pace the territory, its inner and outer floorings, tarmac and concrete and faux-old paving blocks, travertine marble, onyx veneer. It was freezing cold on the barriers and checkpoints. It was hot and stuffy in the piped air of the mall. A net of old terraces had been flattened to build an approach road, though a pub and a corner shop were left standing, to which the guards rushed for their breaks and dinners. A burger van drove up daily, as close to the checkpoint as regulations allowed it, selling butties and plastic cups of tea.

Security guards were everywhere pacing, and yet they had no power really. Their responsibilities were clear to no one: whose laws they were enforcing, and whether it was necessary to obey. Once, a lorryload of stowaways from China made a run for it when the vehicle that smuggled them through Tilbury got held up by the bridge. They ran round and round the development, chased by puffing guards, cheered on by workers watching from the offices above. The real police arrived and took them to the holding station. Every one of the security men on duty that day ended up sacked.

As she smoked, Lorna looked again at the ID card in front of her. She didn't care for the picture much, and she had a feeling she never had. It was a tense face, pinned into a pose that did not suit it. She didn't like the sound of the company she seemed to work for either, and she had a feeling that this, too, wasn't new. She did like her eyes, though; the eyes at least had potential. She gazed at them, captivated, like a baby. She liked her eyes, and of course, her Scottish surname. She liked her name enormously: it spoke of oats, and mountains, and sheep's innards in the starving winters. Lorna liked her name enormously. She thought it was braw.

The toilets were exactly where she had thought they would be, and they were hideous, a marquetry of brownish marbles with a nasty trim. They manufacture the toilets for these buildings off-site, in factories, as whole units; the developer buys them from a catalogue, with ends of pipes sticking out at the corners, ready to be plumbed in. They get transported to the sites on the backs of lorries, then swung into slots in the building's framework. None of these things stopped them from smelling slightly, of ordure and the disinfectant used to mask it. The welds were leaky on the waste stacks, as is so often the way.

This was the funny thing, Lorna thought, sitting on the closed seat of the toilet as she puffed away. Even in her condition, she seemed to know plenty of stuff about the world in general. More than that, she felt fine enough and capable so long as she was just sitting there, knowing things about the world around her, so long as she was just sitting there, looking out. At the front of her head, Lorna felt acute and sharp and clear and clever. When she reached back, though, it went first dim then black.

The outer door swung open, and shoes went squelch across the marble floor. 'Oh, for Jesus Christ's sake, we have a bloody smoking room if you really can't control your filthy impulses,' a voice said, muttering, not quite having the courage to be loud. 'Julie,' thought Lorna, 'for heaven's sake, Julie.' It did not seem to be a happy thought. She sat on until the voice had departed, her cigarette snibbed between two practised fingers, legs raised above the door gap in their lovely boots. She flushed, and lines of little bubbles rose through passages in her brain.

On her way back round the plasterboard partition, Lorna directed herself round the flat beige surfaces by watching for the lilies in their vase. The computers were arranged like sandbags, with books and papers propped up against them. There were coffee mugs with slogans, and plastic coat hangers and old pink folders, and thick rings of souring milk. A poster's corner flapped off a hessian partition. WORLD OF CONFLICT, it said on the legend, under a garish red-and-yellow map.

Lorna could see she was in an office, and given that the blonde girl did not seem perturbed by her appearance, presumably she was meant to be there too. She worked here, in a position of some sort. This, in short, was her job. She had an unknown schedule with unknown tasks, unknown duties and responsibilities. She had a computer on her desk with unknown functions, unknown passwords. There would be unknown friends, unknown fiends, unknown enemies; she herself had an unknown personality. Lorna laughed at the thought of that, though. She had an idea her personality was quite nice.

The computer turned out to be easy. Whenever it asked for a password, she made a deliberate smoothing gesture on her forehead, which seemed to relax a valve or something further back. The password rose to the top without trouble, and was transmitted straight through to her fingers. To log on to the main server, the password turned out to be LORNA, which also worked on the office-manager software. Apart from the email package. The password for the email package was IRUGU5YW.

A new mail flashed up at the corner of the screen: flashing up, Lorna thought, at a moment of danger. It was from someone called Miranda, and it came from within the organisation. It was called Party, with a capital P:

Dear Lorna,

We need to have a chat about the Party. I need to schedule the Guest List by the end of next week. We need to chat by end Monday.

Yours faithfully

Miranda x-x-x

She double-clicked on the calendar icon at the top of her screen: Monday morning, around eleven. Just as she had thought.

'Miranda!' she said, almost to herself, but just a tiny bit louder.

'Yes, Lorna?' The girl from the next desk along raised her smooth blonde head.

'Let's talk this afternoon about this party stuff,' she said. 'Would that be time enough?'

'OK, that would be marvellous, Lorna, thanks very much,' said the girl. Her voice was smooth and warm and dulcet-sounding. Lorna took against it at once.

Another shape was approaching, tall and thin and untidy-looking, with long dark robes and scarves. Her hair was a purply-orange colour, tied back off her face in a pompadour. In her hand she was shaking what looked like a charity tin.

'Fuck me, but if she isn't her own worst enemy, that bloody woman,' she was saying loudly, laughing. 'She is a bloody fucking nightmare. She is. She really is.' She was shouting in the general direction of someone else, out of Lorna's line of vision. She would always have an audience, that one.

A figure rose from the desk on the other side of Miranda, nodding, giggling into a headset. Her hair stuck out from her head in china-bumps. Her trousers were like saddlebags, festooned with flaps and loops. She was jabbing with a stylus at a personal digital assistant. She was like a creature on children's television; her name was Daisy, so that fit.

'Hey, Lorna, I didn't even see you there,' she said, beaming adorably in Lorna's direction. 'Hey, I love that shirt of yours, innit. Can I have it if you die?'

'What a charmer, isn't she, our Daisy,' the pompadour said loudly, as if to Lorna, except that her back was completely turned. 'What a charmer, isn't she, fnur fnur.'

The girl was right, Lorna realised as she wriggled. It was a fantastic shirt, plain but clever, the sort of shirt that doesn't sound like much in the abstract, but moves around with you inside it when it's on. Boring but true, a decent shirt is always worth the two or three cheaper ones you could have bought for the same money. You will feel better, you will look better, and on dull days the heart can be lifted a little by something severe, but with a touch of punctilio to it. It is not the be-all and end-all of anything, but it is a little thing, a start.

The job, presumably, paid for the quality; such a job, therefore, would be quite scarce. She would have to try to keep it, for the moment. She would have to take care.

'Have you heard from Peter this morning?' Miranda said out loud.

'I have,' chimed Daisy, fingering her china-bumps. 'He's in his car, he said? He said he'll be here in no time. That's what he said an hour ago.'

Miranda looked at Lorna, ineffably. 'But aren't we having the afternoon meeting?' she said.

'Well, he's still got time to make it,' Lorna said, looking at her left wrist as she did so. Funny, she thought there would be a watch there. Oh well.

'Have you heard from him, then?' said a further voice: the pompadour woman loomed. Her back hair was tied up with a big black ribbon. She was wearing a baggy velvet garment, as though she needed to be able to hide things, sometimes, at a moment's notice up her front.

'He's on his way, he said to Daisy,' Miranda said, looking wry.

'He is such a fucking loser,' the tall, loud woman said. 'Oops, there goes my dinner money, into the old swearie tin.' She paused to let Daisy and Miranda giggle. There was indeed the sound of a coin or two, dropping slowly on a bed of many more.

'Then again,' the tall, loud woman went on, 'it's always possible that he's off shagging Kelly, innit, making the loser with two backs. I thought I smelt her, smoking in the toilets, but there's a message on my voicemail. This time, she says, she's in bed again with her bloody asthma, as if, I mean to say. In bed with her bloody asthma, as if, I mean to say! She doesn't deserve to have a bloody job, that woman, does she! She doesn't deserve to have a bloody bed!'

'He he he,' said Daisy.

Lorna held her bottom tightly on her chair.

'Anyway, kids, I'm out for lunch, shortly. I'm paying, from the swearie tin, if anyone else would like to come with. A slap-up meal at the hotel de posh, I thought, and with the liquid element playing a prominent part. Monday comes but once a week.'

Her eyes swept humorously round the department, with a special look at Lorna, which Lorna, rightly or wrongly, pretended not to have seen. 'A slap-up meal at the hotel de posh, I thought.' Lorna looked down at her desk. 'Some folks don't know a free lunch when they see one,' the pompadour woman said oddly, in the voice of the noble matriarch in the fifties films. Lorna continued looking down, and the woman walked away. 'I just thought, I'd better crack on with this lot,' she said, smiling brightly at no one and nodding towards her computer. 'I don't know how it happened, exactly, but I'm awfully behind.'

Miranda offered to fetch her a sandwich or something from the shopping mall in the basement, and did she want a coffee, the usual sort or a change. Oh yes, Lorna thought, I know about sandwiches. Pictures arose in her mind on wipe-clean plastic place mats, of thick bready slices filled with slabs of flabby flesh. Miranda lifted a large bag from the corner coat-stand. Daisy picked up a tiny rucksack with a koala key ring. Lorna had the weirdest feeling, of being a person on the threshold of a defining moment of some sort, a bid for freedom, an acceptance of total doom. She didn't know what it was or how it had happened, but she was being given another chance.

The minute she had got rid of the others, Lorna busied herself in determining the limits of her world. Another word for this activity would be snooping, except that she was snooping on herself. She was quick and efficient in her movements, clean and careful. It was like she did this sort of thing all the time.

The nice smart bag was easy. It had keys in it, and a purse with cards, a travel pass, a loyalty card for a coffee franchise. An old brown address book had a picture of a dog tucked into its inside pocket, slinking guiltily across the frame. There were people with her surname, all of them in Scotland; there were other people, in different parts of inner London. Well, they'd just have to wait until later, Lorna thought. She relaxed her forehead and signed her name on a scrap of paper: the writing, thank the heavens, was much the same. She flipped over her software to look again at the scolding email, to read it properly this time, if such a thing were to be borne. It seemed, though, that she had really wiped it. The dolorous email was gone for ever more.

Gazing deep into her computer, Lorna saw the problem turn in the air inside it, an engineering diagram in 3-D. Lines crossed each other and went nowhere. Loops slipped somewhere in their construction and turned back in. Lorna could see no good way out of her present problem except by pretending she didn't have one. She could see no good solution to her brainstorm except to go on as if it hadn't happened, getting on with what she appeared to be doing anyway, in order to see what happened next.

How long could she get away with it? Well, that would be interesting to see. Getting away with it, Lorna thought to herself, with a stream of little bubbles. Getting away with it. What a funny old phrase.

From where Lorna was sitting, the person she would have to deal with most closely was Miranda, and with the mysterious Peter, who, she guessed, sat at the empty desk opposite, its terminal bulging rudely over the divide. She became aware that his phone was ringing. 'Hello, Peter's phone,' she said into the receiver. 'Is he there yet?' said the voice. 'No, I'm afraid he isn't. Can I take a message?' The voice on the other end hung up.

She sat down again, and looked at her phone in wonderment. She relaxed her head again. The number rose from the tops of her cheekbones; she let it flow into her fingers and wrote it down. She stabbed it on the keypad of her telephone. Sure enough, it was the voicemail. 'Hi, Lorna, it's Peter,' said the message. 'It's one o'clock or so. I'm in the car.'

She looked out of her bit of window: a helicopter was toiling across the sky. Directly below, the motorway disappeared into a tunnel with double rows of yellow lights. There was a building site and a housing block and sheets of water, layers of settlement and destruction. She looked hard, she looked away again. She could not for the life of her have explained the structure of what she had seen.

On the other side, the view gave way to a huge construction site with pits and machinery and smoking excavations. Yellow cranes swung great beams of iron. New service cores rose in dull grey concrete with already-rusting iron frames. Beyond, the light was pale and glorious, with cliff-like slab blocks and rolling clouds.

Lorna's eye bounced and bounded across in freedom. 'As Hegel would say, it's a dialectic, innit,' she thought to herself quite suddenly, with an awareness that she voiced this thought quite often, and that she said or thought it because in some way it was true.

'Lumps will rise to the top, my poppets,' the pompadour was saying, trooping back from luncheon with her little gang. 'Lumps will rise to the top, they always do. As evinced, of course, by the example of *moi-même*.'

'I got you your sandwich, Lorna,' said Miranda, approaching with a smart brown bag. 'I discovered a new place, with a more innovative range of breads and fillings.'

'Thanks, Miranda,' Lorna said, peeping into the bag.

'Where's Peter? Isn't he here yet? Do we have an ETA?'

Lorna said that he had left a message on her voicemail, at one o'clock or so, and that at that point, he had said he was in his car. She looked around her and could almost see the secret whirrings. 'Why don't you call him on his mobile?' said Miranda, the very slightest bit plaintive. 'Everybody knows he takes it best from you.'

'OK,' Lorna said. 'Have you got the number?'

'You would think you'd remember it, wouldn't you, the number of times we have to phone him,' said the pompadour woman in a comfortable way. She had a dim old smell of beer

11

or wine to her. She was acting away like mad. 'But that's the weird thing about mobile numbers, isn't it?' she continued pleasantly. 'They're impossible to remember, they have no shape. Unlike the good old-fashioned landline. Which is like a little poem.'

Lorna rang the mobile number, and was clicked straight through to a voicemail service. The other women stood around, staring at her, willing things she couldn't guess.

'You might give Kelly a ring as well, while you're at it,' laughed the pompadour woman, still acting her pleasant act. 'Tell her Julie sends her love.'

'Yes, and tell her Daisy sends her love too, while you're at it,' said Daisy. 'Tell her Daisy sends her love too!'

'I just don't want this week dragging on like last week,' Miranda said, in what was beginning to sound like a whine. 'I just need for it not to drag on. I need to get moving on my party. I need to get my lists sorted out.'

'Well,' Lorna said, spreading out her hands. Hilarious, really. All around her was a desert of empty hills and moorland, and ruined buildings and abandoned schemes.

She sat down and looked hard at her list of emails. There were lots of them, from people and organisations, which she didn't bother to check. It would never matter, no one would notice, she considered, and she turned out to be right. She opened one, though, that looked interesting, having the mysterious domain name of x5wd:

lorna –
re bks: phone me. price list attached.

There was a number, but the attachment would not open. The email was signed 'yrs, rm'.

There was another, from a colleague in her organisation: 'Hi there . . . u OK now . . . Wot abt lunch or something this week . . .' The first name was Harriet, the surname shared with a dynasty of public figures. Lorna looked forward to finding out more.

She quitted out of the email and scrolled down through the folders on the server. She came to a folder called Attn Lorna and double-clicked on that. Inside, there was an article, fifteen hundred words long. It might have been written especially for Lorna in her peculiar condition. It was about multiple personality disorder, depersonalisation, dissociative fugue. Lorna's eye jumped as she tried to read it. A gang of small green aliens hung like little monkeys from the ceiling, laughing at her and chattering, ripping up old pages, chucking them to the ground. Except there were no small green aliens hanging from the ceiling: just white tiles, with every fourth one an office lighting unit, and every tenth a sprinkler followed by a smoke alarm. Lorna looked back at her computer and read on.

Sometimes, the problem is neurological, brought on by injury or epilepsy. Sometimes it is psychiatric, as when sexually damaged children break up their personalities in order to hide themselves in the cracks. 'Leafing over the disparate evidence, however, none of this explains why this problem, and the issues around it, are more prevalent in the contemporary culture,' said the article. One theory suggests that it's the doctors, inventing new diseases so they can publish glamorous research in prestigious journals. Another suggests it's the patients, acting up a bit, in order to get attention, up to and including a moment on daytime TV.

'It is perhaps at least arguable,' the author concluded, 'that this intriguing condition has the psyche of the modern world in its sights. A disease of consumerism and evaded responsibility. A disease of con men, itself the disease of limitless opportunity, limitless desire.' Oho, so maybe that's my problem then, thought Lorna; though really, she knew it was not. How can an 'intriguing condition' have 'the soul of the modern world' in its 'sights'?

Lorna looked again at the article, this time peering. It made you ill to look at it, it really was the most unscrupulous sludgy swill. Lorna shuddered, only half knowing why, as the writing slid from one weak metaphor to another one, not bothering to clarify the relationships between them, garnering evidence about the coruscating nightmare that was the truth behind blah blah. 'I would demure,' the writer said when he meant demur, as if he really had to use such a word in the first place. 'The condition is comprised of,' he said when he meant comprises. Perhaps, Lorna thought, this is where my mind went. Perhaps it took flight and ran away from this man's terrible prose.

'Are you doing the rewrite on the brain thing, Lorna?' said Miranda. Yes, Lorna said, she was.

'Oh goody,' said Miranda. 'I know you'll do it so well.'

Lorna looked again at the writing on the screen in front of her. It really was awful, and it was her job to make it better. Of course.

A dialogue box flashed up on the computer: Save Now? it asked her, and invited her to give the file a name. A phrase came up, clear but tiny, in a loopy lime-green neon, at the very bottom of her mind's black pit: TOTAL DISORIENTATION DISORDER.

That was exactly it, thought Lorna. She typed the phrase straight in.

Chapter Two

Lorna worked on for one hour, two hours, when she noticed that something had changed. A man had moved in on the work-station across from her one. She could feel him loom before she looked up to see him. He brought a great force field with him, of cigarettes and funk.

'My dear girl, the traffic,' the man said in a deep, rich voice when he saw that Lorna had seen him. 'The traffic, dear Lorna, the traffic. You would not believe what it is like.'

He was a tall man, with an odd face, cut off on its way to handsomeness, with not quite as many lines on it as it should have had for its age. He wore a nasty mustardy tweed jacket and carried a canvas briefcase, with the name of an orchestra on it and bits of paper spilling out from its flap. Lorna saw a brochure about mini-breaks, an intellectual-looking journal, a child's drawing in crayon of a person. She felt a mysterious and yet familiar pain of hatred and affection mixed.

'Now,' the man said, positioning his jacket flaps around his office chair. 'Do you suppose that sweet fellow has actually mended my computer this time?' He made to sit, then moved round to prop a buttock on the desktop. 'Why, Lorna,' he smiled, with a charming gesture, slightly out of sync with his words. 'Of course, I meant to say. Thank you so much for what you did last week. You are a wonder and an angel, you know.'

He picked up his keyboard and poked at it a little; sweat gathered, Lorna noticed, in the creases round his nose. 'This bloody machine, I don't know what's wrong with it,' he said, putting it down and standing up again, for all the world like a man who had been working hard all morning and was leaving on a well-deserved break. Lorna raised her eyebrows at him in as pleasant a way as she could.

'Oh, but my dear, I told you, I have to rush off for a moment, didn't I say? But I got those documents, thank you so much. You are such a wonder, you know.'

'So when can we have our Monday meeting?' piped up Miranda, bending her voice round the side of Lorna's desk. 'Peter, it's really important that we have it, Peter. I've got lots of things about the party I really need to run past you.'

'Half past four,' the man said, crinkling his eyes up like a cowboy. 'Half past four, my dears, OK? Half past four, if that's all right with everyone. Half past four. I'll be there.' He seemed to have forgotten he had said he was due somewhere else immediately. He sat down at his desk again and started looking though his post.

Daisy and Julie shot up, like figures on a clock. Daisy bounded over to stand by Lorna, and Julie glided round the back to stand behind him, her long arms crossed. 'Peter, we need to chat about my role within the brainy section,' Julie said, with the look she used to humour idiots. 'Peter, we need a little chat about my role.'

But Peter's phone went at just that moment. 'One second, my dears,' he said.

Lorna watched as Julie stomped back to her workstation, muttering. Daisy seemed to be giggling. Miranda sank back on her chair. Lorna pinned her ears back and pretended to work at her computer. She wanted to eavesdrop but she couldn't. She was laughing so much inside.

Peter's phone call descended into mutters and whispers. 'OK,' he said, putting the receiver down at last. 'See you at half past four, gang. Must dash.' Lorna noticed that his briefcase was still flapping open. She wondered whether to tell him. She decided not.

'He's such a total dish, innit,' Daisy sighed, watching behind him. 'Watch him dive off like that, yeah? Like the Scarlet Pimpernel?'

'Don't you mean that he's just the biggest fucking tosser on the planet,' said Julie, throwing herself back down. 'How much is that for the swearie tin? Jesus fucking H Christ.'

Lorna had forgotten all about her smart cheese sandwich, and her beaker of trendy coffee, which was long since cold. But she drank it anyway, and she ate the sandwich; then she suddenly felt so tired. On her left, Miranda was phoning with one hand while moving her mouse around her screen. 'In the contemporary workplace, it can be helpful to think of oneself as a brand name,' she was saying. 'Every contact a potential contract. That's the important thing.' She put on a squeaky voice with an extra twang to it as she went through the drill again.

Miranda, Lorna noticed, had a special office chair, jointed, like an insect, with integral footrest and wristrest. 'Just the one suit, I find, is adequate for most occasions,' she was saying. 'Office wear through to evening. You can dress it up with a sparkly evening bag, or possibly, a brightly coloured pashmina shawl.'

Lorna looked back through her email browser. Her friend from the famous family had got in touch again:

> This week now impossible, sorry . . . How are you placed next . . .

She was squinting at her screen, trying to think of the right words, when she realised that Miranda was standing behind her, scrutinising her desktop while pretending to fiddle with her hair.

'Look, Lorna, we really do need to have a chat sometime,' she said, as Lorna turned round. 'We really need to do lunch.' This

Miranda seemed to need a lot of things, or else she seemed to think that other people needed to do a lot of things they didn't do. 'We need to talk about the party. You need to run it past Peter, you said.'

'I'm sorry, Miranda,' said Lorna. She was sure she really was.

'Well, it isn't your fault, is it?' said Miranda.

'Isn't it?' Lorna didn't know.

'So can I put you down for a lunchtime chat tomorrow, then? I need to get the guest lists done before I go tonight, and we can go over them together.'

'I'd rather not do tomorrow,' said Lorna, suddenly anxious. 'Can we do it later in the week?'

'That's marvellous, Lorna, I'll so look forward to it.'

Lorna sighed and turned back to her work.

At around five thirty, Lorna realised that the air had changed again. A presence had moved into the corner office, behind the maple double doors. It was Peter, of course, sitting there and smoking, his chair reclining, his feet crossed and on the desk. Lorna caught his eye, looking over. He glanced her back a sternly put question, lifting his wrist and turning his watch to face her.

Lorna looked round and noticed Julie, standing at her desk like a ship's lookout seeking land. 'Meeting ahoy,' said Julie. 'He's moved into the corner office, the fucking bozo. He's started the Monday meeting by himself.'

Miranda gathered up her smart white plastic folder, and her handbag, and a pen. Off she trotted, like a politician at a conference, the folder clutched on her breast. Outside the corner office, she loitered for a moment, waiting for Peter to finish the phone call he had decided to squeeze in. The minute he did so, she knocked on the door and barged in. By the time the others got there, Miranda was sitting on the high-backed chair in the middle, her folder open and her papers sorted, her legs neatly crossed in her short black skirt.

'Does this always happen?' Lorna longed to ask Julie. She didn't ask her, of course.

The corner office was small, just large enough for a little meeting. The desk was big and veneered with walnut; the view from the window was of the river, running away from the city eastwards, as wide and slow-moving, almost, as the sea. There was a beautiful chair, an empty bookcase, and a fish tank, with water and seaweed and seashells in it. Perhaps the fish had not arrived yet. Perhaps they were all dead.

Peter sat at the desk like a mogul. He played the part very well. He raised a finger as the women trooped in and went on listening to another phone call, looking at something, out of sight on the screen. Lorna noticed Julie straining round to look at it. 'He hasn't even managed to switch it on, the moron,' she whispered to Daisy, who laughed. The women arranged their seats in an arc in front of him, like a row of secretaries waiting to take dictation, folders and pens and pencils perched on their knees.

'Right, gang,' said Peter, putting the phone back down on its hook. 'Thanks for coming. Good-oh. The first thing to say is that we're all doing terrifically well, the directorate is ecstatic about the way the brainy section is looking and I had dinner with Bea last week and she seemed really happy. So thanks ever so much to all.'

'Hear, hear,' said Julie, shaking her fists in front of her.

'All right!' said Daisy, like a musician at a soundcheck. 'Way to go! Intense!'

So who's this Bea, then? Lorna wondered, tired and unequal to the task.

Peter dived into his briefcase and came out with a sheaf of papers. 'Here's something,' he said, 'I sat down and wrote last night. Distribute these, would you, dear,' he said to Daisy, and she did. Lorna looked at the document. It was written in two different typefaces, a nice plain sans serif with something frillier at the top. It looked in fact like two documents, one written over the other one. It also looked familiar, like she had written the older part herself.

'Peter, how marvellous,' said Miranda, straining forward in

19

her chair. 'Perhaps my contribution will be useful at this stage.' She swooped among the papers in her folder and produced a beautiful memo, on dove-grey paper, with a smart pink trim. 'I tried to get your approval for this, Lorna,' she said smoothly, 'but as you know, you were never available last week. As you know, Lorna, I needed to get on with it and you said you never had the time.'

Lorna added Miranda's document to the top of her pile of papers. It really was laid out most elegantly, even she had to admit. 'The Party: A Mission Statement' was the heading. 'A Party,' it continued, 'is a Meeting of Persons, a Meeting of Minds . . .' 'Of the devil's party without knowing it,' Lorna thought sourly.

Lorna looked over and accidentally caught Julie's eye. She seemed to have decided for the moment that she wanted to be seen to be enthusiastic. 'Hooray, party time,' she said in a happy voice, her bracelets jangling as she shook her fists. 'Party time. Hip hip hooray.'

'The Guest List,' said the first subheading on Miranda's memorandum. 'The Guest List Needs Accurate Objectives,' it continued, 'if the Party is to Achieve its Stated Aims . . .' The whole thing was written in title case. The layout in general did not bode well.

Peter raised his finger commandingly. 'As I said, everyone is doing marvellously, and the brainy section is looking great. The second thing to say is that of course it can always look better, and Bea seems to be particularly worried about the back end. I think, Julie, you might need a bit more help there, is that all right with you?'

Julie stabbed him a furious look from her chair. 'Well, it would help if that Kelly turned up to work sometimes,' she said, almost spitting. 'She is such a bloody waste of space. She seems to think she's still a bloody stewdie or something. She needs to learn that punctuality is of the essence in a job like hers.'

'Well, as I said, everyone's doing marvellously,' Peter just went on. 'We just need the back end brought into line with the front end, and I spoke to you about this, Lorna, perhaps you could show Julie how you do your little knack.' Lorna looked across at Julie, glowering by the fish tank, her thick dark robes regally folded down the sides of her chair. What little knack? she wondered. What little knack might that be?

Julie stared at the floor with a deep and appalling hatred. She was focusing on one tile of the office carpet, trying to make it burn.

'She's a complete and utter nightmare,' Lorna heard Julie shouting a little later, when the girls were all back at their desks. 'She's a complete and utter nightmare, and let me tell you, I can't be arsed with much more.'

Lorna pulled a piece of paper over the photocopied street map she had been marking up with one of Miranda's highlighter pens. She wondered why 'arsed' didn't seem to count with the swearie tin. Perhaps that had to do with Julie using it as a verb.

It was getting dark, which was a pity, but still. Lorna's mind filled with a survivalist excitement as she planned the route she would take to her flat. It was the flat, at least, whose address was entered next to her name in her brown address book. She was too worn out to be frightened, even. All she wanted was to go home.

Back then, in the mid-to-late 1990s, the spots to which the mad glare of wealth did not extend were beginning to look burnt out and forsaken, although they had looked just normal, only a year or two before. Wealth was getting more intense and more prevalent, and the world shone like television inside it. Poverty was getting more forgotten, more marginal, more squeezed out by the day. Looking at her photocopied street map, Lorna imagined a tall, thin terraced house, with a cuddly husband; an Edwardian mansion block, with ornamental brickwork and a porter on the desk. She could tell from the map it wouldn't be like that. She put her jacket on and her shoulder bag and got ready to go.

'I'll walk you to the lifts,' said Peter, approaching. The smell of funk around his armpits was even stronger. One of his nipples was showing through his shirt. 'I don't know how you stand it, Lorna. You must have the patience of a saint.'

He walked oddly, almost staggering. He seemed to lurch sideways, towards the walls. But he had managed to do up one of the clips on his briefcase. Lorna noticed that he had to swipe his ID card across a sensor before the door between the office and the lifts was unlocked. 'I suppose, if they wanted to, they could be monitoring our movements,' she said, without thinking. 'I suppose, if they wanted to, they could be eavesdropping on us now.'

'Oh, my God, you're right, I hadn't thought of that,' said Peter, looking worried for a moment, until another thought steamed into his head from the opposite direction and knocked the worry from his ear. 'So, Lorna,' he said. 'About my nemesis. I think I have decided what to do.'

'Oh yes,' Lorna said, politely.

'I think, as soon as Bea seems a bit happier with the product, I think I'm going to resign. I think I'm going to move to the country. Children to look after. Poetry to be written. Life to be lived, and all that. You know.'

'Oh yes,' Lorna said politely. 'I think I see what you mean.'

'I shall recommend you take my place, of course, and I'm sure you'll do it marvellously; it's a rarity, a girl like you to have such an eye both for the humble comma and the broad sweep. I shall recommend you take my place, of course, you entirely deserve it. And I really think the best start I can give you in that endeavour would be to get her sacked.'

'I'm sorry?' Lorna said, just as politely. She couldn't think of anything else.

'Well, I for one will always blame my failure on her presence,' Peter said, a petulant shadow coming over his fine face. 'Her work is disastrous, absolutely disastrous. And that desk of hers, it's like a voodoo death shrine, it gives me the creeps just to walk past it. I think she's a fiend, you know. I really do.'

'Well, I don't think you should get her sacked,' Lorna said. 'I don't think that's a terribly nice thing to do.'

'Well, but it might take the pressure off poor Kelly some-what,' Peter said in a musing voice. 'I know the poor girl's hope-less, really, but sometimes that's not the only thing.' He sank into silence as Miranda approached, disconsolate in a narrow coat with a furry collar. 'I've finished the guest list, and I'm coming in early tomorrow to make notes for the eleven o'clock meeting,' she said in her furious dulcet tones.

The lifts were lined in the same onyx-and-brushed-steel effect as the toilets, and plunged down so very quickly, the digital display on the control panel showed only a sinister blur. The ground-floor lobby was vast, high and also veneered in steel and marble, with glass doors as big as the walls of whole cathedrals and a huge, dull-bronze finger sculpture, pointing the way. The mystery was as deep as in the greatest of human temples, only no longer draped and vaulted. The surfaces were hard, broken up with strategic pot plants; the air around them was old and empty. The leaves on the pot plants were hard and shiny too.

Outside, it was cold and dark and windy, but there were little lights embedded in the pavement, marking the way to the train. All around rose ziggurats and towers, with beacons flashing at the top. Lorna stalked on her dinky heels across the open plaza by the waterfront with its rows of split-new ironwork and smooth white shining globes. It was windy and the windows twinkled. She turned up the collar on her coat and ducked behind the pillars into the building's undertow, along a row of arcades. She felt the sharply waisted tailoring holding her upright; she felt her legs all straight and supported in the smart little boots. She felt power and she liked it, and the feeling of simply gliding along a preset track. She sank down the heroic escalator to the under-ground railway, disappearing into a montage sequence in someone else's film.

It's not doing your job well that gets you noticed, Miranda had long since observed, biting at the blunt ends of her side hair as she walked. They only see you when you do something extra, something that brings in added value. So she had vowed from the outset never to get into work at ten in the morning. She would arrive earlier, so her shiny head was already bent over her computer by the time the others got in, making up her schedules, meticulous about the tabulations and the changes from bold to not-bold. Or else she would arrive later, having warned her colleagues the previous evening that she was picking up on a meeting or working on a project from home. 'I can be contacted on my mobile,' she would say, 'if I am urgently needed.' No one actually knew her mobile number. No one ever needed to phone her.

Miranda knew that Peter and Lorna were up to something, and keeping her out of it as usual. It upset her, of course, it very much upset her. But she tried to put her hurt behind her, as she tried to do with all emotions not actively helpful in getting her where she wanted to go. 'It helps in the world outside if you try to rub off your ragged edges,' her mother told her, the time she came home from school in tears and hiccups. To show uncontrolled emotion is to give out confidential information. It's undisciplined, it's undignified, it's dangerous. Someone, sooner or later, will use whatever you gave them to get one up on you.

Miranda worked hard on learning how to control her feelings, making little helpers of them, working with her on the greater goal. At the moment, her voice was her special triumph. She loved its calming sing-song rhythms, buffed and practised, like a piece on the piano, in her mother's front room. She was also pleased with the way she had learned to turn the most ordinary-looking interchange into a shop window of her growing skills. 'Miranda, would you take a look at X, please?' Peter or Julie or Lorna might ask. 'All right, after I've done the A, B, D and Y I have on my list already,' Miranda would answer. 'You may be interested in seeing what I did with the W and the Z also, although I know it was outside my brief.'

Miranda knew where she was going, and she had the next few steps planned out. 'Make a plan, girls, have a map of the future in front of you,' Ms Hamilton the English teacher had told her class at school. 'You can tear it up once you've started, but it's good to have a plan as you go.' Miranda had seen the sense in that idea immediately. 'Shoot for the stars in your ambitions, girls,' Ms Hamilton had gone on a little later. 'Aim high, and don't let anyone put you off.' Although, if it really were that simple, Miranda thought as she lay in bed all wakeful, Ms Hamilton would hardly have become a teacher, would she. She would have been doing something better paid in the private sector, in the media or PR. 'I love teaching, it's my vocation,' Ms Hamilton laughed when Miranda asked her, in her one-to-one careers-guidance session. Miranda looked at her beloved teacher's hippie earrings and decided, with the most enormous sadness, that her beloved teacher was a fool.

Miranda was going places, that was obvious, and she had no doubts about her long-term strategy. But the shorter term was coming to be a worry. In the shorter term, her job was getting her down. There was something wrong with the sight lines in this office. From where she was sitting, she couldn't see the important people, and what was even more problematic, it seemed that the important people couldn't see her. She looked around the office floor sometimes, squinting, trying to determine the lines of power, but instead of a hierarchy above her, all she could see was a fuzzy tangle.

Peter, of course, was her head of department, but Peter was hardly ever there, and even when he was, he spent so much effort pretending he knew what he was doing, he didn't have much time left actually to find out. This was a weakness and left him open to manipulation. Lobby him for long enough, and rather than admit he didn't understand what you were asking for, he would usually give in.

Miranda had exploited this flaw, semi-consciously but adroitly, in getting Peter's say-so for the forthcoming party. 'It's free promotion, effectively, we can do it all by sponsors and partnerships,' she said. 'It's by far the most cost-effective way of repositioning our brand.' 'Of course you're right, my dear,' said Peter, as another thought slammed into his head from somewhere else. 'Of course you're right,' he said, no longer remembering what exactly it was that silly fluffhead was so right about.

Something's wrong, though; something's going pear-shaped, thought Miranda, crunching away on her hair. Something sat on somewhere, some weighty burden; a giant balloon filled up with water, and filled, and filled, and filled. Something's wrong, though, something's going pear-shaped. Miranda could think of nowhere useful to take this thought of hers, so she squashed it out of sight.

But it was Julie and Lorna that Miranda really didn't get. It was as clear as anything to Miranda that something must be wrong with them. Why was everything so weird between the two of them always? Did they not know that the first law of good business is to make of your enemy a friend?

Julie and Lorna, Miranda considered, only had their jobs because they were both a bit older than she was, and so were beneficiaries of an older, slacker system of recruitment. They had their jobs, and they weren't shifting. They didn't have the decency to move over and make way. And neither had much of an eye for accessories, though Lorna, Miranda conceded, was arguably in possession of a certain mousy chic. Certainly she disapproved of the fat bow Julie wore atop of her pompadour. 'Terribly ageing, especially with that heavy lipstick,' she thought, allowing herself the merest cheep of satisfaction as she considered her own no-make-up make-up look.

Miranda sensed that both Julie and Lorna would turn out to be irrelevant to her wider strategy, and at first shied away from too much contact with either. But still, even the toughest of the young and talented needs the help and support of her elders, so Miranda looked around her for a mentor, as her book advised. Peter simply wasn't there enough, so it would have to be Julie or Lorna. She had hoped to have lunch with Lorna tomorrow, after the big meeting; she had very much hoped to bond with Lorna, but Lorna had not made herself available to her. She had tried hard, she had tried so hard, with Lorna. But maybe Julie could be persuaded to do something with that hair of hers.

Perhaps that was just another challenge Miranda would have to take on.

Miranda combed down her soggy ends with her fingers – 'the hairdo of newscasters' as she had once heard Daisy, the so-called secretary, say – and stepped upon the smart new electric train. She was going home to cross-check her draft guest list against the definitive collection of three-by-five index cards she kept in plastic boxes in her bedroom. That was the one thing this job was good for, it was good for building up the necessary networks. It's much easier getting invited to important functions when you have a prestige office-development address.

Once she had gathered as many contacts as she could, Miranda planned to start her own company, somewhere cleverly positioned in exactly the right place. She would build it up until it was ready to go public, at which point, she thought she might sell out. For nearly two years now, Miranda had been dating a tax lawyer whom she had met in a City wine bar, when out with some girlfriends one evening for a quiet Friday-evening drink. The lawyer, she thought, could support her through the lean years of her start-up, then he could manage her finances when it all took off. He bought her a Web domain name for her birthday: mmmiranda.co.uk. He also bought her a beautiful desktop rotary file-card system, retro-styled in solid metal. It was Italian, handmade, a little like a fresh-pasta maker. Miranda loved it. It was the motor of her dreams.

The day after, Miranda took it into the office and filled it with some of the more impressive contacts from her home collection, written out neatly and inserted in their sleeves. Then she started worrying that somebody might steal it, so she took it home again. Then she felt sad that no one could see it, so she compromised by taking it into the office on a daily basis then taking it home again at night. As she sat there on the silvery train in the silvery station, surrounded by other smart people in their stiff black and navy clothes, she could feel the weight of its distinction in the corner of her bag. Like her full-length pink umbrella and her tall vase of sculptural blooms, it was a statement of purpose, as clear as she could make it: Miranda was awaiting the correct window of opportunity, but when it came, she was sure that she would know it. Sometimes, her heart choked with happiness to think of how high she might go.

Chapter Three

It helped that by the time Lorna rose from the ground again in south London, it was completely dark and raining. The darkness hid detail and pushed her mind a little backwards, into what it really knew. Reflections of red and green and amber led her across correct street corners in the correct order. She turned off the street at the minimart like a ghost, as though she were part of the texture of that territory. In the shop Lorna paused, enchanted, at a banked display of sweets in packets. The happy words in the bouncy typefaces wriggled like children, eager to be hugged. She picked up bread, baked beans, a box of milk and a bag of hard green apples. Back the sweets sank in a stupor of grey fat.

The street name in Lorna's address book turned out to refer to a dual carriageway off the main road with no pavement either side of it. On one side there was grass and trees and twinkling tower blocks. On the other, a steep escarpment rose to a great hulk of a dark brown building, windowless and forbidding. Lorna tried to walk along the central reservation, but her feet in her boots kept slipping on the slimy pebble-dash. She gave up and walked on a little path on the grassy bit to the left. It was muddy and wound its poorly lit way along the shadow of a hedge.

A couple of young men approached from the tower blocks,

bent and hooded, their waterproof jackets zipped to their chins. 'Excuse me,' Lorna said, and asked where she might find her building. 'No problem,' one of the boys said, pointing at the second-nearest tower. Lorna thanked him. 'No problem,' the boy said, again.

Lorna ducked round the pillars in the undercroft, through a broken door. The vestibule was warm and friendly-looking. A floor of cracked black-and-white tiling curved through the thick air. The light was very yellow. The lift doors were of steel. The wall tiles were blue with human shapes on them in black. There was a handy sign on the wall in superbly slanted italic lettering:

1–4: FLOOR 1
5–8: FLOOR 2
9–12: FLOOR 3

and so on, to 77–80, on Floor 20. Lorna's flat in her address book was number 81.

The FLOORS 1–19 lift clanked into place and rattled open; a man and a woman, slow and tricky-looking, got out. They crossed the lobby and pressed the button for the other lift marked FLOORS 2–20. Lorna grinned at them politely. 'I'd watch that bag if I was you, girlfriend,' the woman said. Lorna looked, and sure enough, the beautiful bag was coming off her arm. 'Oh, thanks,' she said, over-eager to be friendly. The man wore a tunic from a security company, with a mobile phone like a parrot on one shoulder, buttoned in beneath an epaulette. The woman was wearing leggings and a baggy T-shirt. Her arms were bumpy in the cold.

When the 2–20 lift came, it was cramped and stinky. The man and woman climbed with Lorna, keeping mum. When the door pinged at the top, they got out and started rattling at a door-gate. The building was old now, coming on for half a century. 77, 78, 79, 80, said the numbers in their different styles of writing on their different styles of door.

Lorna climbed alone up a little winding stair to another lobby

30

with a door in it, in a wall of wired glass. The keys worked all right and let her in on a little patio, open to the heavens, its surface bulging, pooled with rain. Brown envelopes were getting soaked in a cage behind the letter box. Plant pots stood forlornly about. One side of the patio was like a balcony, with views to soaking parklands. The other was a sheer wall, the side of the water tank, rising like a sea stack over Lorna's head. It was clad in a dry grey friable substance, neither stone nor wood nor metal nor plastic, some other heroic new material of the modern age. Wet bedsheets thumped and slapped against the side of it, getting dirty in the places where the material was crumbling and beginning to come away. A tiny door opened in a little wall to one side. Lorna opened it and went in.

The flat was in darkness, and the light switch didn't work; but Lorna found a pocket torch, hanging off the doorknob. The first thing she checked was the name on the wet brown envelopes. The wet brown envelopes were all addressed to her. The flat was warm and smelt all right, but looked at in torchlight, it was grim. The hall opened on to a bare-boarded studio bedroom, with a bed in it and a table, made of trestles. Long strip windows gave out to amazing views of the city. One wall was completely filled with books, like a bookcase, except that there weren't any shelves or anything, the books were just in piles. There were fat academic-press editions of philosophers ancient and modern, rational and irrational, most of them shiny and unbroken. There were classics and modern classics, orange and black and black with little pictures, blue and ice-blue and grey-green.

You could tell, though, that this was Lorna's place all right, by the Lorna-sized clothes heaped in cardboard boxes and hanging on nails on the walls. A smart grey trouser suit hung off a hook on the back of the door: just right, thought Lorna, exactly the sort of thing she would have chosen. A beautiful blue jumper was drying on a towel on the floor. The table had an old computer on it, squatting toad-like, and without electricity, dead: Lorna rocked the switch at the back of it to check. The table was loaded with cups, and shreds of tobacco, and bent-up ends of skinny roll-ups, stubbed out on bits of scribbled paper; a cheapo carrier bag was doing service as a bin.

All night, the lobby lighting flooded into her windows through the wired-glass panels. All night, the lift made clanking noises as it ran on its thick chains. All night, the wind moaned and shook the tiling on the roof. The building groaned and made settling noises. She fell asleep once and woke to the sound of drunken singing, coming up a pipe, perhaps, from the flat below:

And it's no, nay, never
BANG BANG BANG BANG
No never, nay never, no more
Will I be a wild rover, a rover no more

She thought she felt her bed tip up from underneath her, sending her, head first, shooting out of the window. She saw all the lights of the city spread out below her, and cried out, unnoticed, as she floated across the top. She wondered if, somewhere, a mother or father was lying awake back in the old country, wondering where she was. She felt small and lost and utterly without social connection. She could almost see the once-loved faces, flying away without her, into the corners of the sky.

In the pale, clear light of morning, the flat looked in some ways better, in some ways even worse. The kitchen, Lorna saw, was dreadful, with rotten mastic and a broken-down old cooker, dark green with its missing control dials, its surfaces black with burnt-in food. The electricity was the sort you charge up with a card you buy at the petrol station and the money on it had run out. But the water was hot and there was plenty of it. She rinsed out dirt and plaster-dust and ran herself a bath. The beautiful blue jumper was still damp, so Lorna turned it on its towel. But she found a clean white shirt, as nice as yesterday's if not nicer, and an ironing board and an iron. A helicopter buzzed right past the ribbon window. A plane flew over from the other direction, banking, starting its impossibly steep descent.

32

It seemed really silly, that Lorna would have to rattle and sink a good seventy metres down the lift shaft in her building, then another two hundred through pipes and tubes and cables before she could commence the ten miles or so she had to go east-north-east. It seemed so inefficient, that she would then just have to take escalators and elevators all the way up again. It would make so much more sense to do such a journey by helicopter, a quick hop from one tall building to another one through the swimmingly empty air. Or what about setting up a cable car between them, a nice little cable car, running on a golden wire.

'You never have to put your hands in your pocket,' Julie was intoning on the phone. 'They pick up the tab for everything on these jaunts. I didn't have to put my hands in my pocket for anything. Free bars in every hotel room, it was absolutely tremendous. Free bars in every hotel room. And that is God's honest truth.'

Lorna looked at the digital display module hanging from the ceiling: it said the time was 10.04. Miranda was bent over her workstation, typing. She looked up unfathomably as Lorna wandered past. 'So did Peter give us an ETA this morning,' she said in her charming upbeat intonation. She had worked so hard to suppress the question mark from the utterance. She had worked so hard on all aspects of her voice.

'He did say he'd be in for the eleven o'clock meeting,' said Lorna. 'He seemed to think it was important to be here.'

'Well, of course it's bloody important,' Miranda said, almost snapping. 'That's why I came in early this morning, to make my list,' she continued, back to her dulcet tones. 'So, Lorna, I've made Peter a list for the eleven o'clock meeting. I was thinking, if he doesn't get here, I could take it in myself, if you want?' The question mark she had been suppressing earlier flipped out now, which from Miranda's point of view was a pity. Questions are a sign of uncertainty and so weakness. By asking your competitor for an answer, you are allowing her to jump in.

33

'If he said he'd be here, I'm sure he will be,' said Lorna. Now what on earth, she wondered, made me want to say that?

The smoking room was just across the corridor from the toilet. It was a tiny room, smelly, with a table and no windows. Poor Miranda, Lorna thought as she sat there puffing. She sensed an easier option there, opening like a tunnel in the air in front of her. She could just do what other people wanted, letting herself be pushed and pulled.

A boy came into the smoking room, wearing baggy jeans and a T-shirt with a Japanese word on it. He smiled vaguely at Lorna but said nothing. A thin woman in scary spectacles followed, scowling over a copy of the snooty paper. 'Oh, it's a fucking disgrace, as usual,' she said to Lorna with a sneer. Her name was Sophie Pottinger, Lorna saw from the ID badge she was wearing; she was the smoking room's champion moaner and stirrer. 'Oh, it's a fucking disgrace, as usual,' Sophie said.

The office before the Tuesday meeting was far less empty than it had been the day before. The population was thickening, bringing with it an atmosphere of ambition and purpose, as people do. They sat at desks, booting up their monitors. They were seen attacking their great toppling piles of post. A dishy young man sat at the workstation outside the corner cubicle, phoning. Standing figures were gathering around him, carrying portfolios, wearing suits. They stood uncomfortably, like tiny models on a maquette: some of them facing each other, confrontationally braced; some of them turning aside, away from the action, whispering and barking into tiny phones.

Lorna stood there for a moment, at the end of the corridor, basking, almost, in the billowing anxiety. The air smelt of body odour and canteen cooking. It was unpleasant, but cosy and familiar. Familiar, from families, Lorna thought. Just at that moment, she felt herself hit by the most wonderful whiff of lavender, with tuberose and narcissus, and just a dainty trace of something dead and rotten in there too. A tiny lady had emerged from the lift and was marching down the corridor towards her, flanked by a couple of the dullest-looking men. Her hair was golden and curly, and she had the most delicate ankles. 'I don't think we can hold on to that much longer,' Lorna heard her murmur, in the lowest, richest rasp.

Lorna excused herself around the grouping and scurried back to her desk. A question skidded round her. 'Who was that?' she longed to ask.

'That bloody Beatrice,' Julie groaned, as if in answer. 'Can't she just go fuck herself over a barrel, the silly bitch.' She crossed her arms and arranged her face into the most peculiar expression. 'Why, hello, Beatrice, good morning, how are you?'

The little lady ignored her and strode over to stand by Lorna. 'Where the hell is he, Lorna? Where the hell is he this time?' Her voice was low and deep, but angry. She said the word 'hell' like an angel would say it, with a wonderfully trilling l.

'We had a message on the voicemail,' said Julie, with some sarcasm. 'He'll be in on time for the conference, apparently. He said he was in his car.'

Beatrice continued to ignore her and went on glaring at Lorna. 'What the hell is going on, Lorna? What is wrong with that bloody man?'

'Look, he's on his way,' Lorna said. 'I'm sorry, but there's not a lot I can do about it, you know.'

The beautiful woman looked at her shrewdly. 'No, I suppose there isn't,' she said.

'I love your jacket,' Lorna added gamely. It had a darling little tippet on its collar.

'Why, thank you, Lorna,' said the lady, continuing on her way. Miranda had taken it upon herself to go to the meeting anyway. Lorna could see her there, on the outskirts of the little crowd around the corner cubicle, looking nervous and puffed up. Lorna could also see that Miranda had seen her and was pretending that she hadn't. So Lorna pretended she hadn't seen Miranda either. She just picked up a pen and an empty folder and wandered over to join the crowd herself.

Beatrice swung past the people gathered outside the corner office with a nod and closed the double doors behind her. Her handsome secretary ran from the printer to the photocopier, distributing sheets of paper among them as he went. He popped into the office, closing the big flush doors behind him. He popped out again. Five minutes, gentlemen, please.

There were women in the crowd, one or two, but no other like Beatrice, like a flower. 'Maybe I could be a ling, a heather,' Lorna thought as she stood there waiting with her folder. 'A scrubby, low-growing alpine. Or a bonnie thistle. Of course.'

Lorna's newspaper had a good name and an illustrious reputation, though the reputation, by the time Lorna got her job there, had long since begun to drop. It had been set up by rich socialists at the dawn of the century, nearly a hundred years before. It campaigned for free education, women's suffrage, wholesale reform of the Poor Law, all the great social issues of its era. The founders had long ago sold the company and moved on to other pressing interests: so many other institutions needing founding, so many impoverished thinking persons, needing to be sorted out.

The more dynamic of the souls clustered round Beatrice's office had an arrowed blur about their outlines. They were only in this office in transit. Even before they had got here, they were already on their way somewhere else. So what if they all had other needs, other agendas. So long as there were enough people buzzing around that office, wanting what they wanted, feeling their painfully felt desires, enough of these energies would inter-sect with one another to keep the thing afloat.

No one spoke to Lorna as she stood there, empty-headed and fraudulent, on the edge of the crowd. No one looked at her, even. The air was thick with bubbles bursting. Everybody had other things on their minds. No one, so far as she could see, was talking to Miranda either, though she didn't want to look straight over. She could see that she was standing with her shoulders back, her chest out, her clipboard resting on a long, flat hip bone by her side.

Beatrice's secretary was actually opening the maple double doors as Lorna saw Peter wander across from the lifts. He was swinging his canvas briefcase from the end of his little finger. He had completely forgotten to fasten it this time, and as he drifted past Lorna, a bunch of papers fell out. 'Miranda, my dear, you are a wonder, thank you so much,' he said in his public voice, smiling with his cheek muscles. 'Oh thank you, Lorna, you are a sport, you know,' he said as she ran after him with his fallen papers; he didn't even look her in the eye.

'Sit fast, wait for the redundo,' Julie was saying as Lorna walked past her to her desk. 'They can't get rid of you, can they? Fnur fnur fnur. Sit fast, wait for a big fat pay-off. Let those fuckers sort it out. Oops, sorry, did I say fuckers there? Next time you come in, the drinkies will be on me from the swearie tin. It's groaning with cash these days, literally groaning. Sit fast, wait for the redundo. Let those fuckers sort it out themselves.'

'Miranda, you said you wanted to run something by me,' Lorna, cross-armed, said. 'Would you like to do lunch today, then?' She raised her eyebrows into her hairline in an effort to look earnest and open-minded. She hoped the eyebrows would make up for the crossed arms.

'I'm doing lunch with Julie today,' said Miranda. 'And I'm in a meeting with Peter about my guest list this afternoon. I'm sorry Lorna, but you said you were busy when I asked you. I need to get moving on it or nothing will happen. I need to be a self-starter, I've discovered. If I don't take the initiative about these things, nothing ever seems to get done.'

'Oh, what a pity,' said Lorna, politely. 'My own fault entirely, of course.' She flipped her screen to look at her newest emails. 'U look a bit weird . . .' said the one from Harriet. 'U sure u OK . . .'

'Fine,' she wrote back, 'just a bit stressed at the moment. How are you? Can we please meet soon?'

'lorna – re phil. ring me – r,' said x5wd's message, with a mobile number. x5wd had programmed his or her email to run with a strapline at the bottom. 'enlightenment means only this – have the courage of your understanding!' 'Kant,' thought Lorna,

'I used to know that. I wonder why I don't have a mobile phone?' A message flashed straight back from Harriet, saying she couldn't do today or this week either as a child had been taken ill or something and she had to go straight home.

Just before one, Beatrice's double doors reopened and the meeting came streaming out. Peter was in the middle of it, laughing, looking surprisingly plausible from a distance. Lorna caught his eye and he waved at her vaguely, the sort of wave that made it clear he wasn't inviting her to join him for lunch. 'Going out,' he mouthed, pointing at his wristwatch. He was surrounded by cronies from the sports desk, and Lorna found the sight remarkable. From the point of view of the Tuesday meeting, he was obviously the tallest and handsomest in his group.

Moving quickly, Lorna nipped over to Miranda's desk and sat down on Miranda's special jointed chair. The sight lines were terrible: she had no view at all of Peter's doings, and she couldn't see a lot of Lorna's, what with the barricade. To the left, all she had was the back of Daisy's computer monitor, and opposite, the absent Kelly's empty desk. Poor Miranda, Lorna thought, it must drive her barmy. Even the orange lilies looked worn out and long-suffering when you got up close.

Miranda's work surface was immaculately smooth and empty, and she had been careful to close down all the files on her screen. But she did keep a set of index cards on a rather ugly rotary filing unit, so Lorna started flicking through. Miranda, she saw, kept unusually diligent records and had a well-disciplined and shapely hand. A jaunty divider marked PEOPLE fronted a section made up of pink and white cards, organised alphabetically by surname. Each card had a person's name, number and job title on it, and sometimes other things too:

NB GAY. Bf Charlie (nb also Nigel !!!!) Man Utd, Paul Smith, buys art. (****art school w/T**** E*** etc, loft S*******)

And another, a pink card with a gold star glued in the top-right corner:

****V well thought of by B (T*** M****** dinner conv); NB
Ptr!!!

At the back of the box was a section marked PARTIES.

Clovis Gallery, 6 May 19**: T***** Group launch. Cheap
white (v busy), A***** McA******* smd to rmbr me from bfr;
approached re job. H***** Z****** v keen on my front!!!!
Sheila, Toby, Charlotte for dinner.

La Ricotta, Price March Hambledon do. Fizz, oyster canapes.
B*** F***, C****** A******* (married to J***** A*****; knows
LORNA)

Delighted beyond expression, Lorna turned back to PEOPLE
and looked up herself:
'LORNA,' the card said, with her address and phone number.
'Joint deputy section editor with JULIE (qv). !!!!!!' it said, ambigu-
ously. And that was all.

When Peter said that thing about Julie's desk being like a voodoo
death shrine, most of his reasons had to do with fear, unscru-
pulousness, the usual boring complex you get when a weak man
feels threatened by a tougher woman. Most of his reasons but
not all of them. There was a truth in there as well.
    Julie's desk was indeed littered with curious and bibelots, like
it was a little shop. She had a tea towel that said WILL POWER
on it, with a picture of Shakespeare, worn like an antimacassar
over the back of her chair. She had a little nodding dog called
Wowser she used to keep spare hairgrips on, arranged like deely-
boppers in two clumps on his head. On top of her terminal stood
the swearie tin, a collecting box with a picture of an African child
on it: SUPPORTING THE FIGHT AGAINST LEPROSY, it said. 'Such

an interesting disease, and so resonant,' she had said when Peter asked her once, trying to be nice and all that, *noblesse oblige*. 'In what way resonant?' asked Peter. 'Well, I was thinking in a biblical direction myself,' Julie said innocently, giving him what she hoped was a pestilential leer.

Every other week, when Peter wrote one of his columns, the paper ran a little picture of him, smiling handsomely, a wise and sorrowful golden retriever, at the top. This meant his picture had been scanned electronically and was stored in perpetuity on the server. So it had been easy for Julie to stash away a copy in the locked folder she kept on her computer desktop, where she performed on it horrible mutilations. She made his head square-shaped and flattened; she stuck it on top of a naked woman. She gave him great whiskers spewing from his nostrils. She stuck his skull with curly spikes.

On her way back from the smoking room, Lorna let her eye slide casually round the back of Julie's computer, over the muddle of padded envelopes, notebooks and press releases, newspapers, and coloured sticky notelets scribbled with heavy black writing. 'BEA4TEA,' she read on one, and leaned forward to look more closely. But the desk next to Julie's was no longer empty. Lorna started and drew back.

A small figure in a big black jumper was sitting there, cringing. A stale smell hung around her, in a nimbus. Her fingers, which she was wringing and wringing, had yellow stains up the sides. She was so fearful-looking, she did Lorna the favour of making her feel fearless. Except that she hadn't done the favour consciously, so as a moral action, it didn't really count.

'Oh, hello,' said Lorna, 'I didn't see you there, Kelly. Are you feeling better? How are you feeling today?'

The girl went on looking at her, mutely. Lorna felt annoyed.

'Well, Julie's having lunch with Miranda at the moment, and I've got a lot to do.'

'Don't worry, Lorna,' said Kelly, cringing further.

Who said I was going to worry? thought Lorna. 'Don't

worry, I won't,' she actually found herself saying as she sat back down.

Kelly had turned up a couple of months previously, by whose offices no one was quite sure. She had been a prodigy at some university in the Midlands; she had already been published in the learned journals. Then something had gone wrong, it had all gone wrong for her. Now she was going to learn how to be a journalist instead.

'I've found someone really bright for the job of Julie's assistant,' Peter had said one morning, bouncing in. 'She's the one with the brightest future of her cohort, they say.' Julie sat in her chair, glowering, saying nothing. 'I've asked her to pop in for a chat on Monday,' Peter went on. 'We can all go out for a coffee and a chat. Obviously I'm not forcing her on anyone. You can see what you think.'

The next Monday, sure enough, there she was in the reception area, sitting hunched on the leather couch in her black turtleneck jumper and her down-at-heel black boots. Kelly was there, but Peter wasn't. He had left a message from his mobile on the voicemail. He was in his car, it said.

Julie took Kelly into Beatrice's cubicle and sat herself down behind the walnut desk. 'I hear,' she said, 'you are a bit of an intellectual, are you, Miss Kelly. I hear you are very fond of reading books.'

'Well, at the moment, actually, I mostly read papers in journals, actually,' said Kelly. 'Papers in journals, mostly. And poems.'

'And what sort of poetry do you like, then?' said Julie, opening her eyes quite wide. 'Pope Alexander? Milton John? Andrew Marvellous? Pam Ayres?'

'At the moment, I read mostly poetry from the German,' said Kelly. 'I am particularly fond of Rilke and Paul Celan.'

'What about novels? What about English literature? I mean, you are English, aren't you, Miss Kelly? English is the language what you speak?'

'Well,' Kelly said, 'I don't think English literature is a category,

41

really. It's a bit parochial and shallow, don't you think? I mean, what is English? What is literature? What's the history of the emergence of this subject? Where does it come from? What's it for?'

'But you are English, aren't you, Miss Kelly? Why don't you just face up to it already? Why don't you just face up to it, Miss Kelly? Do you have a problem with poetry written in your own tongue?'

Kelly looked back at her, bewildered. She knew nothing about interviews and applications. She didn't really know what a boss was, or a team. Being a prodigy at Continental philosophy does not prepare you for working in an office. You learn a lot about concepts and methodologies. You learn very little about weird people in positions of unlikely power, and why it can be useful not immediately to rub them up the wrong way.

'And whoever heard of a philosopher called Kelly?' continued Julie, enjoying herself just hugely. 'Or perhaps you were thinking there, you can be the first?'

Kelly just sat there, feeling awful. Only ten minutes into her first job interview, and already, she must have done that thing she always did, somehow. Only ten minutes into her bright new life in London, and she had somehow set it all off again.

Julie told Peter that Kelly was a disaster area, which in some ways was quite true. 'Well, we'll just try her out for a few months, shall we,' Peter said, as Julie glared at the floor. 'Kelly, my dear, Julie thought you were marvellous,' he told her on the phone that afternoon, when she rang him up from her mobile, on the landing in her digs. It was just as well she had rung him, because Peter had forgotten he had ever had her number. It was incredibly lucky she had phoned him, and that when she had phoned him, he was there.

'My favourite poets are Rilke and Paul Celan,' Julie was at that very second mincing across the desk to Daisy. 'I mean, I asked her, I said, whoever heard of a philosopher called Kelly? I mean to bloody say?'

'Kelly Kierkegaard. Kelly Spinoza. Aristokettle Kelly,' said

Daisy, jabbing with her stylus at the little hand-held game of battleships she held on her palm. Daisy, too, had done philosophy at college, though she had preferred the feminist theory option, especially where it interfaced with the language of the body and so on. She had written a seminar paper, in fact, on body modification and cybersex, and hadn't it been just the biggest load of utter rubbish; not that anyone, including Daisy, particularly cared.

Daisy herself indulged in none of that sort of sad, self-immolating nonsense. Over the course of writing her long paper, events had conspired to suggest to her that people found her body perfectly delightful, exactly as it was. Sometimes it bored her a little, it was true. But in the age of information, as she had in fact concluded in her essay, the deficit could be made up more successfully by temporarily interfacing with ornamentation and small-scale machinery, such as the sleek grey gadget currently resting on her palm.

'You're a veritable cyborg, Daisy,' said Julie, laughing fondly. 'He he he,' said Daisy. 'I'm a veritable cyborg. He he he.'

'Lorna, you know that piece I'm writing for Julie?' Kelly sidled round to Lorna's side to say. Lorna looked at her with an alien exasperation. 'Remind me,' she nastily said.

Lorna had just found a file called Story List, with weekly deadlines in it. It looked fairly full for this issue, fairly empty for the next. The story she had rewritten yesterday was mentioned with a row of question marks after it. 'REWRITTEN BY LORNA,' she wrote in capital letters underneath.

'The thing is, Lorna, I don't know how to get it started. I don't know how to do it. I really don't.' Kelly had a weepy look, from her eyes and from her nostrils. 'I've had the flu, and it's going for my asthma. I haven't been sleeping from the worry. You said, Lorna, if I needed help I could ask for it. I just don't know how to get it started. Please.'

The piece was about why philosophy is still worth studying, in an age of business administration degrees and student loans.

Julie had commissioned it idly, in a cat-and-mouse way. 'Mortality, passion, the death of God, the limits of reason,' she would say to Kelly. 'Speaking as a philosopher, which of these questions do you think is the most important?' She only threw the question out of the side of her mouth, she didn't really want an answer. By the time Kelly thought of something clever, Julie had moved on.

'She said I should call it "Philosophy is the New Rock'n'Roll",' said Kelly. 'But I don't know anything about rock music, Lorna, I really don't. I'd much rather call it "Philosophy is a Lover Too" or something, Lorna. Do you think if I did that, Julie would mind?'

'I don't think it matters at this stage what you call it,' said Lorna. 'I think the important thing is to get it down.'

'OK, Lorna, thanks, Lorna,' said Kelly, shooting up. 'Can I show it to you, maybe, when I've done a draft of it? Can I show it to you for your comments before I pass it on?'

What a hollow victory it is, thought Lorna, getting a person to do a thing you tell them to, when she is so small and defeated-looking, and so utterly devoid of ironical distance. In spite of her brainstorm, Lorna could see very well that Julie's intention in commissioning the article had not been for Kelly to write it. In spite of her brainstorm, Lorna had not entirely lost her nous.

As she wandered along to the smoking room, she passed Kelly, typing on her computer, her body electrified, sitting up almost straight.

'Philosophy is a lover too,' she thought to herself, with an inward cackle, as she sat there smoking. Oh, really, Kelly. For heaven's sake.

'Philosophy is a lover too,' she thought to herself, later on that evening, sitting at the table in her flat, surrounded by a pool of light. She had charged up the electricity card on her way home, at the corner minimart; she bought a spare card also, in case of emergencies and long nights. She had cleared the table of the toadlike computer, which now sat sullenly in a corner, its screen side turned to the wall. She had a couple of back issues of the brainy section in front of her, and she was working her way from cover to cover, analysing its contents and writing them down on a grid. All day, ideas had been bobbing up in her head then disappearing, only their bottoms showing, like little bunnies. She only had such a tiny part of her brain to work with; all the rest of it was in darkness, completely out of reach.

She had a bowl of boiled potatoes with their skins on, garnished with lettuce from the minimart and the other half of yesterday's tin of beans. She sighed and stretched and went to boil a kettle for her hot-water bottle. 'Philosophy is a lover too,' she thought to herself, almost giggling. The heaps of books in front of her were a wall, a tower, tottering to the heavens. The light around her table was a moat.

Chapter Four

What Lorna didn't know, though, was where Kelly got her catchphrase from. She had got it from her professor, a celebrated academic back in those days, before the sort of work he did just suddenly went out of fashion. 'Philosophy is a lover too,' this professor had murmured as he ran his hairy hands under Kelly's waistband. 'Oh my darling. Philosophy is a lover too.'

Kelly's trouble was, she did not understand how she did the philosophy that, apparently, she was such a genius at. She sat at her carrel under the great glass dome of the library, staring, staring, staring at the pages. She got herself anxious, she worked herself up into a state. She thought about the great professor, in his cords, declaiming. And then, her pen was away underneath her. She found herself just doing it, like that.

Kelly doing philosophy was like an artist visited by inspiration. Her entire body clenched up and quivered and became Dasein, or Différance, or the Epistemological Break. She curled round her computer as she was composing. She was an oboist on a sobbing oboe. She was the thinking reed.

'How did you think of that?' the professor would say in the brief tutorials which quickly started getting longer and longer.

Kelly was so nervous, she could hardly speak. 'I don't know, sir,' she said to him, as though she were still at school.

'You don't need to call me sir,' he said gently. 'Call me by my Name.' Kelly could tell he said Name in a special way, with a very particular meaning. The observation gave her a pucker of pudeur.

Somehow, when Kelly wrote her philosophy essays, she homed in on themes and problems in an oblique and witty way, making clever juxtapositions between the apparently quite different work of Aristotle and Foucault, or Hegel and Richard Rorty. Her mastery of the vocabulary was astonishing: German idealism, English empiricism, French post-structuralism, she could do them all. This was because it was not a mastery at all, but a mimicry, a ventriloquism, a way of immersing herself totally then sort of becoming whatever it was that she was trying to understand. Kelly herself had mastery over nothing, not her emotions or mind or body. What she had was intuitive talent, a marvellous gift in its own way, but one that needs a strong will looking over it if it is not to go wrong.

A couple of days before an essay deadline, Kelly would start getting tenser and tenser, more and more miserable and anxious, as she sat there cringing, thinking about Historicism after History or the Politics of Politics, or some other mysterious phrase. She stayed up all night, drinking flat supercola and picking at her eczema, opening new rows of sores on her chest. Then at last, the night before the final deadline, inspiration would descend, a stony angel. The essay came together like poetry and she'd just type it up and hand it in.

'The task of Enlightenment is this: have the courage of your understanding!' she wrote on the title page to her summer-term long essay, 'The Impossibility of Pure Reason: Kant, Blanchot and the Deconstruction of Courage'. Her argument was valid in many ways, and the way she put it together was droll. But like all her work, it lacked proportion; it had no comprehension whatever of the relation of parts to the whole. It was immature and yet impressive, in a weirdly lit way. It was just the sort of thing that made a splash in the learned journals of the time.

'I think you should submit a paper from that one,' the tutor said, lost in admiration, fingering the odd little cleft on his chin. 'Philosophy is a lover too, you know,' he murmured later on that very evening, fingering at her.

Now the voice possessed the body of Kelly in ways other than the philosophical, everything seemed to change. Kelly had been cold and alone for as long as she could remember: she still got jittery when she thought about her poor old panda, dry crumbs of rotten rubber dribbling from the places where the fur had split. But now, she had a warm hulk in her bed of a morning, the bristles she could not tell from blackheads and the scary dead look of his jaw. 'Life suddenly took over,' the professor mused in the bar at the conference, after delivering the keynote lecture. 'Life just suddenly took over,' he wept, on his knees, to his wife.

The wife got hold of Kelly's number, and started phoning and phoning, screaming about the children, telling her to tell her husband he had no bloody right. 'Oh dear, it's the mad wife again,' Kelly would murmur as they lay there, listening to the machine. 'Doesn't she know that, philosophically speaking, there's no such thing as rights, really, we only have freedoms, which are provisional and which we must constantly defend?'

'She spent far too long sucking from my life all the joy and beauty,' her lover said, pushing at Kelly's head. 'She spent far too long sucking from my life all the beauty and the joy.'

The professor thought Kelly had the mind and the soul of a philosophical poet, and brought her his old Chatto & Windus Rilke, with parallel translations by J.B. Leishman and Stephen Spender, which they read together, aloud:

And you yourself, how can you tell, – you have conjured up
prehistoric time in your lover. What feelings
whelmed up from beings gone by! What women
hated you in him! What sinister men
you roused in his youthful veins! Dead children
were trying to reach you . . .

The professor watched, entranced, as his voice grew big and round against the thin white wall of Kelly's study bedroom. Kelly sat there, watching him, her soul inside her baying adoringly, like a little dog.

Kelly didn't know she was good-looking in the way that, if she had gone to Hollywood and had a makeover, she had the basic bone structure to be a star. She was just a student in jeans and a jumper, with cheapo ankle boots or whichever trainers were on the Sale rack outside the nearest shop. Lorna did notice, vaguely, and spent nearly a minute of her hard-pressed time imagining what Kelly might look like if encouraged to sit up straight and get a decent haircut. But unfortunately for Kelly, the main people who looked beyond her turtle jumper were sexually predatory old men.

The mad wife had some sort of a grip on her husband. The professor stopped returning Kelly's calls. She got herself drunk on alcopops and rang him up at home. 'Kelly, Kelly, you don't want to be this sort of person, do you?' the professor sorrowfully said to her. He put down the phone so gently on its cradle, then pulled it straight from the wall.

The strength Kelly had found in philosophy vanished without the structure of the university behind her. She no longer had sections to prepare for seminars. She didn't know what to do with the stuff she read. Philosophy itself, she felt, had deserted her, and seemed to have eloped with her fragile genius. The pair of them left behind them a cold and shapeless world.

'Who, then, among the ranks of angels, will hear me when I cry?' thought Kelly. 'Who, then, among the ranks of angels, will hear me when I cry?'

A couple of months later, the professor came to London to give the headline lecture at a sell-out one-day colloquium at the ICA. At the dinner afterwards, he found himself seated next to Peter Pevensey, the noted poet and commentator in the press. Pevensey the Pathetic, the professor was wont to call him, throwing his execrable articles across the room in fury. Peter Pevensey,

Peddler of the Banal. The professor had even thought of citing Pevensey in his lecture, as an example of the bland, mediocre, fundamentally dishonest work encouraged and rewarded by the English cultural class system. When he found himself sitting next to the bloke at dinner, though, he was glad that he had listened to his wife when she had suggested it might be more politic, in the long run, if he took that bit out.

The vile Pevensey mentioned that he had just taken on an executive role at a famously failing liberal newspaper, setting up his own department to produce and edit a pull-out supplement of essays and ideas. 'A sort of think tank,' was the way he put it, 'all very collegiate, you know. Of course, one is really more a writer than an editor, but it's difficult to refuse these offers when one gets them. They seem to want one so much.' Part of his brief, Pevensey went on, was that he seek out bright young talent for the department. The professor thought of Kelly right away.

'She is a great mind, according to the professor,' Peter said proudly as he introduced Kelly to the others. 'Her papers have already been published in learned journals. So hopefully we'll see you writing things a little bit less clever for us, my dear. As you can see, we're absolutely thrilled to welcome you on board.'

Kelly looked at the faces gathered in front of her: Julie, she saw, was smirking, then put on a blank look, copying her own.

'Who, then, among the ranks of angels, will hear me when I cry?' thought Kelly. 'Who, then, among the ranks of angels, will hear me when I cry?'

Since her heartbreak, her concentration was too shot for systematic reading, but she still looked at the poetry books the professor had left behind him, which she had taken down to London with her in her bag. She no longer had the attention span to follow Rilke's argument through death and into the inner mysteries, but she knew there were sepulchres in it, and steles, and dusty urns. She gazed into the pinhole eyes of the sombre gentleman on the cover. She murmured to herself a bit in the German that was printed on the left-hand page:

Und so verhalt ich mich denn und verschlucke den Lockruf
dunkelen Schluchzens. Ach, wen vermögen
wir denn zu brauchen?

'And so I repress myself, and swallow the call-note / of depth-dark sobbing,' goes Leishman and Spender's sonorous translation. 'Alas, who is there / we can make use of?' 'Who is there?' Kelly thought.

Every day, Kelly came to the office wearing the same black jumper, the same grey jeans, the same black ankle boots. Over the weeks, the jumper got more bobbly, the jeans grew more and more grey, and the boots got scuffed and crooked. Also, Kelly had given up on bathing. She washed at the sink in her room but she didn't like to take her clothes off in the shared bathroom out on the landing. The chipboard door fitted badly, with huge gaps at top and bottom. You would lie there naked in the water, with dirty strange lads smoking joints around the payphone only a couple of feet away.

Peter did vaguely wonder why his protégée was not shaping up in the way he had expected. She didn't look like a prodigy somehow, not when one thought about it that one knew, exactly, what a prodigy even was. Then he remembered something he had completely forgotten, and the thought of Kelly was gone. 'Yes of course, my dear, you're right, of course, absolutely,' he was saying down the phone line, his mouth half full of chocolate cheesecake. The sweat was blooming in his armpits. His head was thumping. His eyes were red and sore.

If you looked hard at Kelly, you could still see pinkish flushes beneath the black swaddle and the greyish miasma. You could see a sparky, enthusiastic person, in need of a bit of support and guidance, in need, perhaps, of a friend. She wasn't a stupid girl; in many ways, she was the opposite. This is a mistake often made by bad businesses, thoughtless people. They can't see beyond the surface and the short term of people and of things.

People say they buy papers for the news, but also, they are seeking out something else: something that makes them feel better

51

about themselves and their place in the world around them, something that gives them a bit of hope. The hope is both consumerist and utopian, in a dialectic. It is about dream holidays and anti-ageing products. It is also about signs, through what is available, of optimistic life. That's one reason journalism became so personalised in the 1990s, with all those articles written in the I-voice under a little picture of the writer's face. It's the cheapest way of presenting an image of a world in which people are fully valued, supported in their individual enthusiasms. OK, so not everyone gets the special treatment, but at least such a thing as a special treatment exists.

Kelly's employer had forgotten, even, about this sort of phoney caring; not in any case that Kelly would have been a pampered star. But the error was anti-human and also anti-commercial. Readers sensed the despair of the enterprise, the loss of hope and faith. One by one they gave up on that particular paper and moved over to buy the spoilt and snooty one instead.

When Lorna woke up on Saturday morning, the light was clear and glorious. As she watched, a sparrowhawk soared up past her window, pointing, cruciform, in its special darting shape. She followed it up to the heavens, where it was joined by another bird, the two of them making their way as a pair. Far away, on the eastern horizon, a silver tower winked on in the sun.

Lorna's head ached after a week of sandwiches and too much coffee. Her mind was filled with flat, bland desktops and sheet after sheet of blurry text. In the kitchen, she drank a glass of tap water and put on the kettle and raised her head and looked out of the kitchen window, forcing her eye muscles to go wide. There were three blocks the same as hers at angles along an axis, and they were very handsome: white and slender, with long, smooth ribbons of oblong windows. The roofs were ornamented with great barrel-vaulted water tanks, faced with glass. It was like looking out over a sea or something, a sea of grass and trees and tall ships. It really was a vision of a better way of life.

According to cuttings kept in the library on the precinct, the estate Lorna lived on had been a model to everyone when the first keys for the first flats were handed over to their tenants in 1955. It had been one of the London County Council's first post-war developments, and it had benefited from such a pent-up rush. 'The excuse that better building "would cost too much" can no longer hold good when we have seen what scientific application, proper organisation and considered use of the machine can produce for destructive purposes,' her own paper had written in a famous editorial of 1944. 'It needs little imagination to realise what could be done for housing by harnessing this power for constructive purposes instead.'

The energy, the money, the great ideas had pretty well dried up by the time Phase III went up in the early 1970s, as represented by the penitential slab of systems building across the canalised main road. But Phase I had intelligence, and idealism, even, though idealism in social policy can be a dangerous thing. Excellent young architects in the council offices drew the monumental shapes and massive volumes they had seen in photographs from Germany and the Soviet Union. Bold use was made of new materials, precast cladding, reinforced concrete, pressed-mineral fireproof tiles. A mural was made for the wall of the estate's very own branch library, in the Contemporary Style then fashionable, out of pottery shards and fragments of broken bottles. The name of the estate was spelt out in blue italic writing on the side of the shopping precinct, by the outside stairway leading up to the residents' social club.

There were four little flats like Lorna's, one on the top of each of the towers, prefabricated hut-like structures, tucked between the water storage and the hauling mechanism for the lifts. The architects had stuck them on as an afterthought, as studio bedsits for single working girls. A brochure in the library archive showed them on utopian diagrams, paper spills dressed in wide belts and demiwaves, serving pickled olives and fish-paste hors d'oeuvres from rhomboid plates. The flats themselves were only a bedroom really, with no cupboards, no shelving, no storage space to speak of. The fifties girls would open a tin of soup for their supper, when they weren't dining out in night clubs with their boy friends. They would rinse out their smalls in the bathroom and go to the launderette once a week. Where they kept their little suits and gowns, though, was a mystery, thought Lorna. Perhaps wartime caused the architects to forget how much a working girl does need to ring the changes with her outfits, to keep herself dainty and fresh: the subdivided drawers for hosiery and underthings, the deep shelf at the top for her hats.

Lorna's intestine gurgled in misery. She might as well have half a sack of flour, mixed with lard, just swilling around inside her. She drank a glass of water with lemon juice in it and then another glass, straight up. She put on scruffy trousers and a pair of trainers. It was time to procure some plain, harsh food.

Past the library and through the precinct, Lorna passed under an arch of housing and skirted around the side of another square. The buildings here were clad in wood with wide, deep ground-floor verandas, completely enclosed in mesh. There was a recycling point surrounded by walls and sloping concrete, then a side street of pretty Victorian terraces which once upon a time had been slums. Then it was the high street, with its building societies and chain stores, crammed with baby buggies and electric wheelchairs. The pound shops had out their bargain-label disinfectant and purple buckets. The Turkish shop had a tumble of rude aubergines spilling down its front.

In the supermarket, Lorna watched as her basket filled with potatoes, leeks and carrots. 'Broth mix,' she thought, seeing a packet of dried rice and peas and lentils. So she bought that too. Oats went in, and a bargain-label brown wholemeal, and a small slab of orange Scottish Cheddar. Just in time, she remembered washing powder for the laundry. A tiny lady watched over her basket while she ran to get a nice big box.

She walked back to the flat the same way as she had come, leaning forward with the weight of her laden rucksack. The sun was out and the birds were tweeting. A gang of kids was wreaking harm at the recycling containers: the air thrilled to the crash of bottles propelled through portholes, the crunch of trainers on broken glass. A boy on a skateboard thumped and slapped across the concrete, limbs like scissors, his body bouncing. Lorna's arms were stuck out stiff, like handles, dangling a plastic carrier on the end of each. On the approach to her building, she walked over cans, carrier bags with knots tied in them, the slimy bones of a precooked chicken. Someone had upended the giant bin that collected the rubbish from the waste-disposal chutes. Someone had left a puffed-up nappy and a half-full beer bottle standing by the wall.

In the lobby, she found the man she had met on her first night in the building, loitering in his beige nightwatchman tunic, the phone tucked in under the epaulette on his left shoulder now matched by a cigarette packet tucked in on the right. Lorna smiled at him and said good morning on her way to the odds lift, which was already sitting there, open and waiting. 'It only goes up to nineteen, you know, mate,' the man said, reaching up for a cigarette. 'Oh, I don't mind walking, it does me good,' said Lorna brightly. The man shifted his weight a little and looked at her like she was mad. Back in her flat, Lorna dumped the food bags and emptied her rucksack, then filled it up with her dirty laundry. Life was very full for the bachelorette in her London penthouse. Life was very full indeed.

She was stuffing her sheets into the giant dryer when she became aware that she was the focus of attention from a person, a creepy peculiar feeling at the back of her neck. She turned round, angered, and saw a young man, sitting on the seating, pretending to read a super-trendy magazine. He had sandy hair and a nice face, white and bony with pale freckles, and he was wearing baggy jeans and an enormous parka. She didn't mean to stare back at him, but by the time she had thought of this, her face had already moved and stuck.

'Hey, Lorna,' the young man said, when he saw she'd seen him. 'Hey, Lorna, I thought it was you, right enough.'

Lorna smiled, for something to do.

'Robin Moody,' the young man said, thrusting out a hand. 'You may remember, we met before. And you're Lorna, are you no, and you are doing your laundry, as am I.' His voice was Scottish and full of humour in that special synthetic way you often hear with Scots who have moved to London. They manipulate the level of Scottishness according to the person they are talking to, how much they can get away with, what sort of an impression they think it fitting for the occasion to make.

'I'm sorry,' said Lorna. 'I was right in the middle of it. Sorry, Robin. I really am.'

'I didn't think you lived around these parts,' Robin was saying. 'I had you down for an Islington sort of person. The trendy North London media chick.'

'Oh my goodness me, no, Robin,' said Lorna. 'I live in those flats over there.'

'Do you? Do you? My auntie lived in high flats like that,' said Robin. 'My auntie, remember, my favourite auntie, I told you about her that time. Oh look, you've got a paper. Can I take a butcher's while you're putting your stuff in the machine?'

'Go and get your own one,' Lorna said, without thinking.

'OK, I will then,' said Robin, with a grin.

He ducked out of the launderette and, for a moment, Lorna thought he had gone. She caught the eye of a pretty woman, packing sheet after sheet into a huge striped bag. 'Your boyfriend, he go quickly!' she said. Lorna smiled and said, 'Doesn't he just?' Then he was back, with a plastic carrier from which he thrust a soft-drinks carton with a straw. 'I am absolutely sure you'll be a big fan of this,' he said.

Robin Moody was one of those pale, bony Scottish men with a hint of iron under their surface: tough bones in his skull and skeleton, metal fillings in his teeth. His face was both friendly-looking and objectively strong and handsome. His accent was west coast and gregarious, and came and went in a manner at the most half conscious, as often happens with Scottish people when they find themselves adrift. 'I am, you might say, a militant modernist,' he would say to women at smart parties, on those occasions he had managed to blag his way in. 'No to mention a dropout of an ancient Scottish university. If you can make the two compute and all. If you like the cut of my jib.'

Robin had been a star at his ancient Scottish university. The cut of his jib was immaculate, and he was acclaimed as a bit of a genius, the writer of forbidding essays in which he explored those dark spots in the modern canon where the pieties of mere literature most explosively gave way. Robin, it was said, really did understand what the post-structuralists were on about, and the post-Freudians, and the post-Marxists too. And he was always happy to explain it to his fellow students, particularly if they were of the female persuasion, and pretty, and quite posh.

Robin at university was famous for the cut of his jib and for the brilliance of his essays; and then, on the first day of the final examinations, he suddenly dropped out. He wrote his name on the answer book, and something else, which had been disclosed to no one. And then he got up and walked out of the examination hall and straight down to the betting shop, where he put £500 he had borrowed from his favourite auntie on a dog. He won his bet too, so then he had three grand to play with, which he spent on rare vinyl, small press poetry books and American magazines.

Ever since he was a teenager, Robin liked buying things and collecting them and swapping them, in deals that he considered gave him an advantage overall. He did it with records, he did it with books and comics. His jib was always superior to that of his cohort. He knew the market and he had an eye. The London financial firms were full of men like him, keen and greedy, except that the City boys were whizzes at sums and calculations, and Robin had never bothered much with the numbers side. He preferred being paid in cash if at all possible, which was one reason he stuck to books and records, although the storage was a problem and the margins could be small.

But Robin Moody did know an awful lot about his books and records, and there's always a place in London for a guy who knows his stuff. He was particularly deft with underground culture, surrealism and situationism and so on. This was fine when this sort of thing had a popular revival, at a public gallery or on television, but was getting harder and harder in between times and, Robin judged, the market overall was in long-term decline. What stuff there was available had long since drifted through the markets into the hands of the people who most wanted it. There simply wasn't an awful lot more to find and sell.

London, Robin discovered, wasn't easy, even for a character such as he was, attractive and resourceful, a lad of parts. Journalism, he thought, would be an idea for him. He wrote well, as he had proved at university, and what with his compendious knowledge, he had lots of ins, he thought, to the world of books. You would have thought so, wouldn't you, but he didn't. In the London literary environment, people were in the habit of thinking that they had already known everyone who counted for years and years. It was difficult for an outsider to get a toehold, even such a star as Robin Moody. He sent out his emails and it was as though he simply hadn't. No one even bothered to reply.

'The cheapest tea in south London,' Robin said in the café. It came out of a huge steel pot, wielded by a man in a dirty white overall. It was thick and stewed and bitter, and the cups were none too clean. The counter had a plastic case with cakes in it, large and lardy with dull white icing. Robin ordered a cheese bap and a Scottish biscuit, out of a box on the sill. 'I can't get over you living round here, round my bit,' said Robin. 'You always seem so much the north London trendy media chick.'

'Don't call me a media chick,' said Lorna, crossly. Robin chuckled and Lorna smiled.

'Did you think again, about getting me round?' Robin said, digging into a pocket in his parka and drawing out a scratched old shag tin. Lorna did not know what he was talking about, and said so. Robin rolled tobacco in a paper between his fingers then offered her the freshly made cigarette.

'Well, I mean, I can understand if you're no eager to part

with them. Personally I'd no part with my philosophy books myself.'

'Oh, so you're that dealer on the email who keeps inviting himself round to my flat?'

'That's right,' said Robin, giving her a look of hurt and covetousness mixed. 'So much for any idea I had about making an impression, right enough. But as I say, I understand if, on reflection, you're no so eager to part with your collection. A girl like you needs her Hegel, after all that stuff that you were saying, that time we met before.'

'What was I saying about Hegel, pray tell me?' asked Lorna, teasing.

'All of human life is there,' said Robin in a copying-Lorna voice, 'the struggle for survival. The struggle for survival and the struggle for meaning too.'

'And the meaning is the struggle, don't tell me?' said Lorna, recollecting. 'And meaning is survival, too?'

'Well, it's a dialectic, innit,' said Robin, 'As you were always saying.' He lowered his eyes and looked up at Lorna, and the two of them laughed and laughed.

Lorna had the feeling that in some way not entirely to do with her brainstorm, she had known this man before. It might have been that she was meant to meet him. It might have been because he really did look like someone else. Or it might have been because he was quite good-looking, really, so did in fact look like most of the men you saw in advertisements on the television and in the celebrity magazines.

Or maybe she really had met him a long time ago in the old country, perhaps she had even known him well. Perhaps Robin had even been her boyfriend at some point, or if not Robin, then someone very like.

Back in her flat, it was getting late and Lorna was overcome by a wave of panic. She was alone and lost and without resources. She really didn't know what she was supposed to do next. She plugged in the toadlike computer at the wall, but it was broken.

It seemed to be gathering itself for a flicker at one point, but then it just went phut.

She went to the kitchenette to see if the pot was boiling. It was, so she threw in cabbage and potatoes and cooked them down to a khaki mush. It was delicious, served with soy sauce and a dash of mustard. As she ate she went through the old brown address book with its dreary thicket of people's names. Dim notions came, of happiness and sadness, simplicity and difficulty, but they were dim dead notions only. The only names that lit up at all were those of Robin and Julie and Peter, glimmering with hints about power and past lives.

She turned to the piles of paperbacks and picked out the Hegel Robin Moody had mentioned, J. M. Miller's translation of *Phenomenology of Spirit*, an ugly pinkish paperback, bound up in sticky tape. The binding cracked, there was a sweet, neglected smell, a couple of pages split off. But then, the book fell open at one place, line after line marked with a pencil. It was the famous short section, 'Independence and Dependence of Consciousness: Lordship and Bondage', often called 'The Master-Slave Dialectic', for short.

Lorna started reading; it was strange. The lumbering half-translated German rehearsed a terrible power struggle between two individuals who were not people so much as potentialities, sonorous mud-creatures, fighting it out for supremacy in the swamp. Death is involved, a fight to the death, each conscious-ness staking its own life on the death of the other. But neither dies, there is nothing interesting about a bloodbath. They survive to become two opposing forces, Lordship and Bondage, and then they fight some more, bound to each other just as much as they fight to get away.

Then the great switch happens. The Lord, who seemed all-powerful, is revealed as a secret weakling, bratty and wilful, too spoilt to be able to manage on his own. And the Bondsman, for whom everything was hopeless, has an all-conquering hidden strength. 'For this consciousness has been fearful, not of this or that particular thing or just at odd moments, but its whole being has been seized with dread; for it has experienced the fear of death, the absolute Lord. In that experience it has been quite unmanned, has trembled in every fibre of its being, and everything solid and stable has been shaken to the foundations.'

The vocabulary was horrible, a flabby pudding of mad molecules, except for a few plain words, which glowed, fluorescent, in the failing light. Lorna took care to see that she was sitting up straight, and read on. A passage had exclamation marks pencilled in all the way down its margin. A deeper understanding, a deeper upset, floated past her eye.

'Through work, however, the bondsman becomes conscious of what he truly is . . . Work is desire held in check, fleetingness staved off; in other words, work forms and shapes the thing. The negative relation to the object becomes its *form* and something *permanent*, because it is precisely for the worker that the object has independence . . .'

The light was fading from the profligate windows; with a click, the interior lobby lighting came on. Lorna moved in her chair and recapped on that last bit:

'Through work, however, the bondsman becomes conscious of what he truly is.'

Chapter Five

'But really, it all has to go phut somehow,' Peter continued. 'Did you see that graph they did of our circulation figures? Really, it all has to go phut.'

Sitting on a high stool, the strap of her bag wound round her ankle, Lorna felt the thrill of the city rising in her gut. She had a Martini in front of her, with a green olive and a witty onion. She was in a bar of turquoise blue and stiff brown leather, surrounded by prosperous young people in pointed collars and narrow coats. She sipped from the steep, straight sides of the Martini glass; a fizz-bomb of herbs and liquor hit deliciously the side of her head. This was the life, a drink in a bar in the City of London. She watched herself sideways on the mirrored pillar by their table. Plates of olives and salted almonds were surely on their way.

'Of course, old Bea was desperate that I come along to help her. And it all seems to be trotting along quite well, don't you think?' Peter's forehead looked pained. 'They're still turning a profit, you see, Lorna. They're still turning a profit, even though the business is in decline.'

'So why bother?' said Lorna, enchanted by her onion, sitting there on the end of its little plastic sword.

'Well, why do you bother? Why does anyone? Lorna, look, Lorna, people have their reasons for pretending. We all do. Including you.'

Lorna sat on, being silent. Peter's foot touched hers, still keeping guard of her bag. It did not seem polite to flinch immediately, so Lorna kept her foot there for a moment, then moved. Looking at this man, she thought in a way that she sort of liked him. She could see that he was a lovely man in his way. He was a fish out of water, obviously, going flop flop flop; but he was a fine-looking fish, a fish that had really stood for something once, a heraldic dolphin with human lips. He was a gentleman amateur, adrift in a ruthlessly professionalised environment. He was a lonely stag in a world increasingly built on a scale for nippy little rodents like herself. She imagined him, picking up his noble hooves over annoyingly little walls of thin plasterboard, trying to manoeuvre his barrelly body round corners strewn with spikes. She could run rings around those bony legs if she wanted to. She could dart through the passageways with ease. The drink, she realised, had exploded warmly inside her. Lorna laughed and laughed again.

'But you'll have lots of fun when you take over,' Peter said, nodding at a waitress who brought the bill along on a little metal tray. He slapped down a shiny credit card. The waitress bobbed and smiled.

'You can't imagine the half of it,' thought Lorna. She had her plans, she was sure, even though she couldn't quite remember them at the moment. Keeping silent, in the meantime, was her secret skill.

But Lorna was sorry to hear it would all go phut shortly. She had almost forgotten about her brainstorm, what with the magnificent vistas she saw ahead of her in life. She felt like a person without problems, sometimes. She was just beginning to get into the swing of things, she thought. The brainy section worked on a weekly production cycle, Monday through to Friday, getting more and more pressured as the week went on. Mondays were easy days, for planning and meeting and phoning. The girls were supposed to research stories and phone up contacts. Then they were supposed to come together at the Monday meeting and fight it out, with Peter adjudicating. That way, the brightest, freshest stories would be assured of coming to the top, was the idea, really. That was the way you got what was known as a 'mix'.

It sounds fine in theory, and it might have worked, had Peter been in the habit of letting the Monday meetings happen. But Monday was Peter's day for hardly ever turning up at the office, and so, they seldom did.

Miranda was easily best at the telephoning. Lorna watched her in a marvel. When she took over, she'd put Miranda on the phones all the time. She had her lists she kept clipped to her folder, she had her rotary index-card system; she made one call, she made another and another. She listened to her voicemail half-hourly. She checked her email, she noted things down from the Web. She went through piles of other papers. She had her little stock phrases: 'Just checking in', 'I'll take a raincheck', 'Just touching base'. As the day wore on, her voice would get louder, her phraseology more and more reckless. Brittle, pent-up Miranda underwent a metamorphosis as she was more and more taken over by an outrageous bonhomie.

'Oh Andrew, you bad man,' she would giggle. 'Playing telephone tennis with me all last week.'

'A nice Chardonnay, oaked or unoaked,' she continued. 'A nice Chardonnay, or maybe a bone-dry Chablis for a change.'

'Lucinda!' she went on, almost crowing. 'I have to apologise to you fulsomely.' Eavesdropping from her own desk, Lorna smiled.

Beatrice's adorable PA came over with a message. Julie was beset with shooting pains in her wrist and lower forearms, which she called 'me RSI trouble', making a point of saying 'me' instead of 'my'. The pains were supposedly a repetitive strain injury, caused by spending too much time working at a keyboard, though Lorna found this unlikely, in the light of how little work at a keyboard Julie ever seemed to do.

Actually, when Julie rang in to complain of 'me RSI trouble' and so on, what she generally meant was that she had a problem with the students to whom she leased her spare three-bed council flat. She had bought it for a song at the beginning of the 1990s, when they were going cheap to sitting tenants, and moved out to a nice little house straight after. The flat was forever getting burst pipes and leaky radiators, and the students were forever phoning up. Anyway, Julie had woken up that morning in considerable pain from her RSI trouble, and had gone straight to see the physiotherapist. She would go straight from the physio to her lunch appointment, according to Beatrice's adorable PA.

'Poor Julie,' said the adorable PA, grinning. 'That's the third time in a fortnight, innit?'

'The fourth, I think, Daniel,' said Lorna, grinning back. 'She suffers for us, innit, don't you think?'

Lorna loved finding herself in the boss position, assigning pieces, correcting proofs, sorting out problems, when she could. She watched her staff, she got to know their strengths and weaknesses. SEE ME, she wrote on a page proof, like a schoolteacher. She was almost singing sometimes, she felt so light and strong. It was, as Peter had said, a rarity to be such a girl as she was, with an eye both for the humble comma and the broad sweep. It's such a joy to find the thing you're good at, and then to be allowed just to do it, all day long.

'Daisy,' she said, when her red marks had become unreadable. 'Can we go over accents in French again? They don't go on consonants, look, they go on vowels, apart from one, but not the one you think it is.' Daisy laughed delightedly; she knew her written language was hopeless, that was part of her charm. Soi-distant, inter alien, costa nostra; she kept lists of her best mistakes on her personal digital assistant. She did not use punctuation hardly ever. When Daisy wrote a sentence, it just went on and on.

A page proof landed on Lorna's desk, from Miranda. PERFECT PANACHE AND MORDANT WIT, the main splash headline said. 'But you can't put "mordant wit" in a headline,' Lorna said. 'It's horrible, it's just horrible. No one's going to pay a pound for a paper that says "mordant wit".'

'I meant mordant in its original Latin sense, of "biting",' said Miranda. 'The wit is biting because it is sharp. But I'll change it if you want me to, Lorna. Really, it's entirely up to you.'

Lorna watched Miranda, wearing her sullen face, call up the headline file on her computer. She highlighted the word MORDANT and replaced it with SEARING instead.

'Lorna,' Kelly sidled over at lunchtime, bringing a faint smell of wet bins and old potato parings with her in the air around her jumper. 'I'm nearly finished my article now, Lorna. I'd love it if you could look it over, Lorna, before I hand it in.'

'I'm glad to hear that, Kelly,' said Lorna, not looking up from her work. 'I can read it in a minute, if you like.

'Lorna, I don't know what to do about Julie. She wouldn't look at me yesterday when I tried to speak to her about it. I think I must have pissed her off in some way.'

Lorna closed the file she had been working on with a sigh. 'Well, I don't know, Kelly, I haven't heard anything about it. But you were late again yesterday morning, weren't you? Do you think that might have something to do with it?'

Kelly pissed off Julie in so many ways, that was the trouble. Kelly was just the sort of person who pissed people like Julie off. She was so often late for work in the morning, and instead of being smart about it, saying sorry once then putting it behind her, the lateness hung around her cringing body right the way into afternoon. 'Oh, for fuck's sake,' Julie would say, scowling. 'Where has poor little Kelly been this time?' Kelly didn't seem to notice that the question was sarcastic. It was her asthma, it was her flu, it was a problem on public transport. Julie herself was late also, every other day, if not more often. But that was no help to Kelly in her position. If anything, Julie's lateness made Kelly's position worse. Also, Kelly's work was completely dismal, 'on the odd occasion,' as Julie put it, 'that she actually deigns to come in'. Being a genius at philosophy doesn't make you an accurate proofreader. Or, as Julie liked to put it: 'For someone supposed to be such a bloody brainbox, she really is a bit of a useless spaz.'

A little later, Lorna watched as Kelly edged across to Julie and said that she was sorry she had been late so many mornings, and that this time, it really wouldn't happen again.

'No, no, don't give it another thought. Please, don't give it another thought,' said Julie.

That was a bit unkind, thought Lorna. It meant the business remained unfinished. It meant Kelly could not put her lateness behind her and move on.

'Did you look at those proofs I gave you?' Kelly then asked Julie.

'Yes, yes, they were fine,' Julie answered. 'Just a few tweaks, you know, which I'll get somebody else to sort out.'

'Couldn't I do it if you mark it?'

'No, I think it would be quicker if I call somebody else in.'

That was unkind cubed, really, thought Lorna. It meant Kelly would never get to see where she was going wrong.

And there were the computer problems. Kelly was constantly crashing and losing stuff, even though she had been told repeatedly to save her work every quarter of an hour. 'I'm sorry, I forgot,' she would say, looking up from inside her jumper in her drenched and tragical way.

'Oh Kelly, really,' said Julie, her bosom growing as she lifted her arms. 'How long have you been here now?'

Hypocrite, Lorna thought. She had seen Julie many times, staring straight in front of her, rigid with anger, because she had got her own computer stuck. A gentle young man from IT leaned over her, trying to help her, making faces to himself about her unconscionable fury, her looking daggers, her fear.

Daisy picked up her phone. 'It's a laddie called Robin for you, Lorna?' she said, in a saucy Scottish accent. Lorna picked up her receiver, twisting. Julie, she noticed, was on the other side of the office, deep in conversation with Lady Beatrice, laughing richly. Lady Beatrice was laughing also. Strange.

*　　*　　*

Lady Beatrice – for such really was her title – was not the actual head of the whole operation. The actual head of the whole operation was the editor-in-chief, a small, quiet Yorkshireman with thinning hair. He was seldom seen at the northern end of the office. He spent his time dealing with the bigger picture, business plans, PR campaigns, figures for the year. Beatrice was only the executive editor, a position that involved less commitment and yet was slightly more powerful, in a way that no one quite understood.

'So basically, she's the editor's deputy, then,' Lorna said to Peter in the cocktail bar; Peter, with a pout of gleeful mystery, shook his head. 'Old Bea isn't deputy to anyone, she would see that as beneath her. Old Bea always pleases herself.'

Beatrice, it was hinted, was paid the most exorbitant salary for her services. And yet, it was also suggested, she had a lot of her own money in the company, which was how she came to hold the position she did. She was some sort of an heiress, or maybe the money had come to her by marriage. But the point was, she had it, which was the important thing. She had been seen wielding a putter on the roof of the investment bank across the inlet. She had been seen stepping in and out of sports cars, Concorde, private jets.

Beatrice moved in the highest social circles, which was seen as being good for the newspaper in a way that Lorna did not understand. She sat in her office, gossiping on the phone with other important and stylish people, comparing notes on who was well thought of, who was rated, who was in with whom. She sent her PA across the floor to summon senior editors to her office. She had a basket outside her door in which department heads deposited the week's page proofs for her approval; Beatrice had to see every page before it was printed, and to send a page to the printer without her say-so was a dire offence. Even Peter had to stand like a little boy outside her office as she lounged backwards in her handsome chair, running a pen along her diary, swinging her legs in their neat slacks and cute little loafers, tinkling with laughter on the phone.

The rich, Lorna noticed, have many more friends than the poor do, or at least they get invited to more parties. Every day, Beatrice's adorable PA printed out her schedule, taking care to write CONFIDENTIAL at the head of it in double-letter-spaced caps. He would then ensure that spare copies were left lying around the laser printer so that passers-by could pick them up. Lorna marvelled at the lunches in restaurants and parties in art galleries, book launches, movie previews, gala dinners for such-and-such a famous person or in aid of something else. There would be rice cakes with slivers of pink fish and wilted seaweed. There would be napkins instead of towels and signature pamper products in the loos.

On Friday afternoons, Beatrice had to leave the office espe-cially early in order to get to Scotland for the weekend. It was her habit to drop her corrected page proofs on people's desks just as she was leaving, demanding rewrites on headlines, stand firsts, captions. It seemed to Lorna inefficient that Beatrice told people what she wanted only on the Friday teatime, as she was leaving town. It meant that Lorna, Peter and Miranda had to work until close on midnight, sometimes, pulling all their work apart and doing it all again. Surely Beatrice could look at the plans on Wednesday or Thursday? Time and time again, Lorna asked Peter to put her thought to Beatrice. Time and time again, Peter seemed to forget.

It was well known in the smoking room that Peter had been hired by Lady Beatrice, on a whim more or less, because she fancied him. 'Everyone knows he's always been hopeless,' said Sophie Pottinger in her pawky way. 'Everyone knows she only hired him for his pants.'

'Shame for her, then,' said an older woman, looking up from a pile of letters. 'He seems so devoted to those kids of his. Don't you think so, Lorna?' The woman smiled a basilisk smile.

Lorna, actually, could not imagine Beatrice doing anything so humble as fancying another being. And as for loving them: surely not. Love had too much in it of necessity and huddled bodies. Beatrice surely lived in an environment too rarefied for love.

'To a great extent,' Peter mused to Lorna in the bar that evening, 'Old Bea is the newspaper. And the newspaper is old Bea.' Lorna passingly thought of the dreadful writing, the smelly toilets, the little men and the angry women. Perhaps she was missing something, what with her brainstorm. She thought for a moment and she wondered, but she didn't say a word.

'It's a bit like Hegel, Lordship and Bondage,' Lorna said to Robin Moody the next day in the spaghetteria in Soho. 'It's a dialectic, innit, like Hegel says. I'm the one who's working, which means I'm the one that's getting the workout. I'm the one who's actually learning stuff, about myself, about the world I live in, about the boundaries between the two. They aren't learning because they're just dozing. They're getting me to do all the work for them, and it's making them go soft.'

'I wonder about you sometimes, Lorna,' Robin said, widening his vowels in his sly way, 50 per cent entirely conscious and 50 per cent maybe not.

Oh, he was almost perfect, thought Lorna, fainting. He had such a good dark Celtic anger in him, and he had just had a most excellent close haircut. He was wearing black trousers and a nice dark shirt with a button-down collar. The spaghetteria glowed red and flaming with surfaces and candles and pitchers of cheapo wine.

When Lorna and Robin met at the spaghetteria, they didn't do the London thing of cheek-kissing as a greeting. There was an air of discomfort about that which might simply mean that they were both from a cold proletarian country where people didn't do that sort of thing. Robin was already sitting there, like he owned the place, when Lorna got there. Lorna almost felt for a moment that, in fact, he did.

The lady came and stood by Robin's side, smiling. 'I'll have a pasta whore,' he said to her, handing her back the menu. 'That's a whoreson pasta. That's what I always have when I come here. Now. Did you bring me a paper, like I asked?'

He looked at the front page, he licked his fingers, he sat back and crossed his legs. 'It's such crap, Lorna,' he said, indicating that week's cover story. 'It is not authentic. It is not creative. I don't know why a nice girl like you is wasting her time.'

He wanted Lorna to squirm, and so she obliged him. There was a thrill there, the invasiveness of the questioning. It was a small frisson.

'I do it,' Lorna said, 'for the money. I've told you that before.' There was a long, long silence. Robin looked at her, glowering.

'And also,' Lorna added into the silence, 'it is interesting, sort of. It's good to be a part of something. It's good to see how these things work.'

'But I mean to say, isn't it just the biggest heap of bollocks?' said Robin. He read out a snatch from poor Peter's weekly column. 'It's trivial crap, it makes people stupid. Look at it. It's fucking cack, right enough. Who is this moron Peter Pevensey? He's fucking disgraceful, so he is.'

'He's my boss,' said Lorna laughing. 'He is fucking disgraceful too.' She told him about the Monday meetings, the spilling brief-case, the mysterious relationship with Lady Beatrice. Robin watched her face throughout. 'But,' she said, 'also I like him. He has his heart in the right place in some way.'

The lady, Lorna thought, gave her a funny look when she came round with her pepper mill. She wondered how often Robin Moody came in to eat his whoreson pasta, and what sort of people he usually came in with.

'The whorish pasta is really excellent,' said Robin shrugging, 'but really they're all good, it's a fine wee joint for when all you fancy is something plain. I've heard tell, you know, of this lovely Beatrice. Is she no just a silly airhead spoilt wee bitch?'

It was still not clear to Lorna how Robin lived, exactly, though politics of some sort appeared to be involved. He signed on, and maybe he was ashamed of that, Lorna wondered, which would be understandable at his age. She knew he knew all sorts of peculiar people, from his trading activities and what he called his networks; she knew he had books he kept in a storage container,

71

waiting for the day he would have a home to put them in. She knew he was house-sitting for some guy he knew on one of the gentrifying old streets of terraces by the Elephant & Castle, not a million miles away from where Lorna was living in her flat. She knew he had a mobile number he seldom answered. She knew he had a Web-access email, and that was more or less that.

Lorna wondered if drugs did not figure somewhere among the Robin Moody portfolio of occupations. Drugs as much as politics would explain the surprising social connections, plus, he was one of those men who always carried a lot of cash about. Lorna did not like the idea of drugs at all, especially for someone in her currently ambiguous state. She looked at Robin hard in the light of a scraggy red candle, trying to see what it was she sensed in his steely framework, under the button-down shirt and the flat-fronted trousers and the pale freckled skin.

'Why,' Robin said with a sharp look, 'are you wasting your life like this, trying to read other people's minds?'

'I'm not trying to read people's minds,' she replied sulkily.

'Yes you are. And you probably can do it too. But it's limited and it's slavish. Besides which, I'll tell you something. You'll never, never catch up.'

The minute they got out of the glowing spaghetteria, Lorna started to gabble, out of shyness and a sort of fear. He said, what a life she had, such fantastic views in front of her, between working on the wharf and living in her building. He said, she should have a party in her flat and ask her colleagues, and Lorna laughed, appalled.

'But that's you right the way through, so it is, you separate work and home much more than you need to,' said Robin. 'You have an unusually pronounced sense of privacy for a media chick, I've noticed. Maintaining that marvellous Lorna mystery. Oh, I know all about that.'

'Don't call me a media chick,' said Lorna.

'Sorry, hen,' said Robin, with a grin.

As the place Robin was living in was so close to Lorna's tower, they might get a minicab, he said, from the office on the corner.

Lorna said that a bus would do her fine. 'OK, a bus then,' said Robin Moody, making sure his arm brushed lightly on her coat. 'OK, fine, then, we'll get a bus then,' he said. As the crow flew, the place Robin was staying was fairly close to Lorna's tower; but it was on a different road south from Whitehall, a different bus route, and so, a different stop. There he was, though, still standing there, looking down the way, towards the river, and humming a Scottish tune. 'There we have it,' Lorna thought vaguely, slinking slightly. 'Arrows coming at me. Statement of intent.'

It was nice for a change to be caught up in someone else's volition, warm and supported. It was like clinging to the end of the swimming pool, by the place where the heated water bubbled out anew.

'But why,' said Robin shrewdly, 'does a lassie like you, with a good job, a media chick, excuse me, stay in a place like that in the first place? Could you no have found yourself a rental somewhere a bit more salubrious?'

'I suppose,' said Lorna, 'I'm trying to save up a bit of money, for a deposit on a flat, you know. I suppose I'm fed up of living like a student at my age. It's not that easy, you know, buying a place to live in London these days. It's pretty hard to manage financially on your own.'

Robin was walking her from the bus stop through to her building, down the side street behind the Georgian terraces, behind the fifties brick housing blocks, to the bit where the buildings went pale and flat and thin-walled.

'Do you really think it was ever easier?' said Robin Moody. 'All that bohemian shite, living for a week on carrots and a pack of Woodbines. Because I don't, not really, I think it was always a big fat lie. I think that people who lived like that got money from their parents, still do, and they always did. They just pretended that they didn't, and wrote daft articles in the Sunday papers, like all that crap you sub. And a fool like you, you fell for it, the great way-out boho dream.'

'Whereas a fool like me,' he said, 'I know I have to work my way. I know it has to be me who does everything. I know it's only me who gets things done round here.'

'Well, I mean, I support myself and everything,' said Lorna, flustered. 'No one's giving me secret donations. It's all just me.'

'In a day and age like this one, it's no enough to be good at what you're doing,' Robin said authoritatively. 'A person needs to have war aims, you know, a sense of direction, you need to know what you want. Cos if you don't, you'll be manipulated by predators. Manipulated by predators, right enough.'

'What a nasty way of putting it,' said Lorna. 'I think I work bloody hard.'

'Yes, but there's something a wee bit passive about you, Lorna, something a wee bit blank. You seem to think that if you just sit there, renting your wee flat and doing your wee job, and working really hard like I'm sure you do, one day it's all going to transform you; and I put it to you, Lorna, that so far as I can tell, it never has got you forward before this and it isn't going to now.'

They walked in silence past the plastic mesh that fenced off the dodgy little park; Lorna wondered whether to mention her brainstorm problem, then decided she should not.

They came to the forecourt by the lock-up garages that formed the base of the huge brown scissor block across the road from Lorna's tower. It was dark and cavernous. Lorna would not have gone that way on her own. They crossed the road and skirted a broad car-parking area with at the far end of it a pub. An illuminated path wound away from the street round the undercroft of the towers, towards the shopping precinct under the concrete bridge. A man walked down the path, carrying a television in both arms, like a baby. A burst of karaoke power ballad came from the pub.

'I suppose,' said Robin Moody, 'as a resident of one of our esteemed welfare state's largest high-rise housing developments, you're part of something bigger than yourself just by staying there. Ha! How many folk joined to you by the same lump of concrete?' He flung his arms out as if about to join in the singing, but pushed open the broken swing door instead. The rubbish bin was overflowing, as usual. A comb, a string of beads and a bashed-up handbag lay strewn across the ground. 'It's scary here,' said Robin. 'I'm not letting a wee lassie like you go in there on your own.'

The light was yellow in the lobby, very yellow and thick-aired. It felt all wrong for Lorna to be on the threshold of her building with a man she had met in the world outside. The chequered floor rose up to meet her like a time tunnel, the normal dimensions no longer pertaining. Far above, Lorna could hear the dull nag of an alarm bell. 'The lift's stuck,' she said, turning from the odds one to the evens. She felt incredibly self-conscious. Her voice was weirdly damped.

'There's this couple I keep meeting in the lobby,' she said to Robin, gabbling from shyness again. She told him about the phone and the cigarette box, buttoned in under the flaps. She told them how the couple came all the way down in the lift from the nineteenth storey, just so they could go all the way up again to floor twenty. 'Imagine that, being so completely dependent on these crappy lifts, Robin. Imagine that, not being able to walk a single flight of stairs.'

'Oh, but that's chronic,' said Robin. 'What is the world coming to, right enough. All folk need is a bit of self-discipline, Lorna. All folk need is a bit of old-fashioned pride.' The lift came, Lorna stepped in and Robin hovered. 'I have to go up,' Lorna said, 'and you, you have to go home, I think, don't you?'

'I'm no going,' said Robin, gallantly. 'I'm going to lie across your doorstep all night and keep you safe from harm,' he said. 'I'm going to be your loyal wee dog.'

'Oh, please don't,' Lorna said, half smiling. Robin grabbed her hand and raised it to his chin.

She felt a fluttering, and among it, the click against her knuckle bones of strong, sharp, iron-filled teeth. The light in the lobby was yellow and bent round; the tiles stretched and foreshortened, and seemed to double up. She felt exposed and obscurely excited. She couldn't tell overall yet if this was a good thing or a bad.

Chapter Six

The lift stopped at the fourteenth floor and, sure enough, it was the weird kids Lorna hated running into, twin sisters, entwined in their matching hoodies. They held to each other far too closely and looked over, smiling and pouting in the most peculiar way. Lorna smiled back briskly, letting her eyes go crossed. The deferential lady came in next, with her clingy son; the two of them cowered straight into a corner. A shoot of Lorna's being reached out in panic in the dark. The lift thudded on ground level and opened its doors to a flash of daylight. Lorna shook herself, bounded out of the building and hurried across the grass.

It was a gorgeous day, though, so when she got off the train at the wharf, she decided not to take the smooth white tunnel into the basement, but to let herself rise on the steep, steep escalator until she came out on the ground. New building was beginning between the station and the tower; a sort of jetty stuck out into the water, clad with the same paving stones as the surface thousands of people tramped twice daily, on their way in and out of work. So was this ground she walked on, thought Lorna, or more water? She stopped for a minute and looked about her. The way between herself and the land beyond was blocked by a blank blue hoarding. She peeked through a crack and saw an enormous hole.

A team of men in hard hats and yellow jerkins were working on the base of the tower, testing the exposed joints of the structural steel beams. Tap, tap, tap, the first man went with his little hammer, shouting out figures, which the second man wrote down. A third man followed, probing at the fastenings in the gullies between the panels of the skirting. 'Routine checking procedure,' he said when he noticed that Lorna was watching. 'Routine checking. You never know.'

The development was designed to make a splash from a distance, and from one of the two main angles along the grand concourse from which, the architect calculated, important visitors would approach. From the walkway round from the station, however, it looked like any ugly office building, with fire vents and dry risers and a gap at ground level in the cladding, stuffed with bits of bag and packets and bashed drink cans. Lorna loved coming at the wharf this way, at an angle, round the back and sides. You got to see the edges, the oddities, the errors. It was like being a Borrower, being in the same world as the usual one but on a different plane.

She passed through a shiny bulkhead, past signs banning dogs, smoking, workers in protective clothing. The doors opened silently as they sensed her coming, then closed again to protect the cosy air. It smelt of breakfast food, coffee and fresh-baked muffin mix, always slightly undercooked. Breakfasts were different here, thought Lorna, sweeter-smelling, easier to chew; much more fun than her own drear oat flakes boiled in water, with raisins for interest and a small, dry orange on the side. Life in general was more fun in here, on the inside, getting your nails done, eating sushi and fresh-squeezed juices, tripping along the shiny pale terrazzo floor. You would never see a join if you didn't want to; you'd never need to decide things, so long as you stuck to the script. It was like living inside a television screenplay. Your feet would never have to touch real dirt.

A group of men in blue security-company shirts were standing by the hideous bronze finger sculpture in the ground-floor lobby. 'Wharfinger,' thought Lorna, stopping again as she realised the connection. 'Wharfinger. Of course.'

Just then, Lorna noticed Daisy scurrying ahead of her, her long thin legs with bold blocks of shiny black shoe on the ends of them. Swallowing an urge to duck for some reason, she ran to catch her up.

Tap, tap, tap went a man outside with his hammer; one of the great glass panels shattered in a way it should not have done.

Within an hour, a sheet of thick tarpaulin went over it, secured by its enormous eyelets with nylon rope.

When Lorna got into the office that morning, Miranda was compiling the final guest list for the party. 'I'm holding all calls,' she said, importantly. 'I'm checking over my RSVPs.'

Lorna picked up a pretty folder that had landed on her in tray, marked for her attention from Miranda. It was a dossier of newspaper cuttings with the phrase 'mordant wit' highlighted on each, in bright pink pen. 'Thanks for this, Miranda,' Lorna said. 'Has anyone heard from Peter this morning?' No one wanted to be the first to giggle or make a face.

Lorna would find it difficult to say whether Thursday or Friday was her favourite. Thursday had subtle colours in it, a sense of preparation, before the disorder and emergency that came with the end of the week. Today was Thursday, and so the desk had a quiet hum. Although the appearance of collective purpose was an illusion. Most data input was on emails, the stirring up of issues against colleagues, the organisation of leisure-time events. But the criss-crossing activity was just enough, in just enough of a balance, to keep the day aloft.

Kelly, Lorna noticed, had been in early and was already working that morning when she arrived. Her body was looking quite different. She had started sitting up straight. Lorna suspected the reason she was there so punctually was because she had been working right through the night: she was surrounded by cola cans and sweet wrappers, and her fingers were all stained. Kelly was too entrenched in the bohemian ways of students, Lorna considered, working all night on things at the last minute, manipulating her metabolism with caffeine and sugar and heaven knows what else. She needs to reset her body clock as an adult, thought Lorna. She would suggest it, tactfully, when she got the chance.

Even Miranda, for once, seemed happy. 'Hi there, Miranda here,' she said as she picked up the phone, her voice smoothly dropping, like white chocolate. Miranda was doing her social sculpting, shaping her great event. Ambition and longing glittered in the air around her. The party would be the cumulation of Miranda's life's work so far.

Lorna, too, felt excited as she booted up her computer. She loved the way the pages came to the desk, electronically, through plugs and cables. She loved the shapes of the letters, the way they leaned into one another to make words. She loved the way the words made phrases and sentences, and somewhere in that, the miracle of meaning, lucidity and purpose: the possibility of structure, the possibility of hope.

They were working that week on Peter's pet project, a double-page pullout done in partnership with a pressure group, about civil war in Europe and the forced, exhausted movement of peoples over lands. The pressure group supplied the copy: 'Besnik was 12 when they came for his father.' 'Suzana was eight months pregnant when ordered at gunpoint from her house.'

'Did Peter say anything yesterday, about being late in this morning?' said Lorna, to the desk in general.

'Did he ever?' said Miranda, almost laughing. 'Will he ever again?'

Lorna looked at her screen and clicked on an icon. It unfolded to look like a spread in a newspaper, exactly as it would when printed, although at this stage it was only an idea really, an idea made of light. All the boxes were there, for pictures and text and headlines. They were stacked up against each other, filled with nonsense writing. A small box with big letters in it was a headline. A big box with tiny writing in it was for text. Starting with the huge framed gap that would be the page-lead picture, Lorna checked the structure to see that everything was in its place. The structure was fine, the possibility of it coming to hold meaning. The possibility of it coming to hold meaning. This was Lorna's job.

It was still not clear to Lorna how the work was supposed to be divided, but she had a good grasp now of what the team as a whole was supposed to do. Peter commissioned the pieces, mainly. Then it was everybody's job to make them fit on pages, with pictures and headlines, and then to make them shine. You wrote headlines and captions that made dull stories look exciting and full of purpose. You filled the gaps with wit or depth or indignation. You did whatever it took to make a reader see a civilised, cultivated product, to make them want to be a part of that world. You did whatever you thought you could do to make them want to hand over that pound coin.

The edges of boxes shimmered when you picked them up with your cursor; looking closely, Lorna felt a little sick. She ran her mouse over a story in a document, picked it up with the cursor and dropped it into its box. She cut out the little knots of space that stopped the text from flowing freely. She highlighted it again and changed the type size. She loved watching the blocks of text flow around the page until they bobbed and settled, great icebergs on a sea. There was a beauty there and a dignity, regardless, almost, of what the article said.

She had her big page-lead photo, she had fetched it from the picture desk. It was a shot of a hut interior in a holding centre, overcrowded, with thin, untended faces looking up from blankets on bunk beds.

HEADLINE HERE IN 48PT
PLEASEY PLEASEYYYY

the fat black letters said in the headline box: the headline flipped over two lines, which meant she would have to find a phrase that both looked nice and tidied up the sense enough when split in the middle.

WHAT A WASTE OF TIME
THIS IS, RIGHT ENOUGH

she wrote in over the top.

She looked at it for a moment, pleased. The letters glowed as they bounced along the computer screen, full of life and brains. Then she cut it out and wrote a proper headline, taking a quote from the article and blowing that up big:

'I CAN'T SEE ANY FUTURE
ANYWHERE ANY MORE'

It did its job.

Quickly, she trimmed the text to fill its row of boxes, cutting out all the on-the-one-hand-on-the-other-hands, the fact that, the empty words no one knows the meaning of, 'inculcate' and 'extirpate' and 'aver'. As she cut, the computer sutured behind her. Where there had been an ugly sprawl of verbiage, there was an actual story about something, clean and neat. Lines of power surged and flowed through Lorna's little corner as she watched the words and pictures scud across the screen to fill their boxes, without words spilling over, without ugly bits of white space.

Not even Beatrice could want a change on this page, Lorna thought to herself when she was finished. It was such a thing of beauty. The letters, the shapes and the meanings merged perfectly. She had made a new whole out of a heap of rubbish. She closed the file, well pleased.

Kelly, she noticed, was slinking around behind Julie's desk, pretending to be looking things up in the dictionaries. Julie, meanwhile, was on the phone, plotting, probably, pretending she couldn't see that Kelly was there. Sure enough, when Lorna looked back at her computer, there was Kelly's article, sitting on the server. Lorna took the quickest peep:

'Twilight of the Idols; A Treatise Concerning Human Nature; The World as Will and Representation. Ever since I was a teenager, I wanted to be part of whatever it was that was inside those big books with their forbidding, important-sounding titles . . .'

It was all there, in sentences and paragraphs, with a pertish rhythm. The article did not look totally disastrous; Kelly hadn't written a ghastly bit of poetry, or a dolorous confession, or an academic essay by mistake. Lorna's relief was great, and surprisingly personal. 'Hey, Kelly,' she called over in a nice voice. 'I'm looking at your article. It's really, really good.'

Kelly smiled back and went red.

A page fell on Lorna's desk from Miranda. DYING FOR HELP: that was the main headline, over a picture of refugees on a rocky hillside. The women had long skirts and scarves over their heads, but that would not be enough when night drew in or the weather changed. CULTURE VULTURES, said the strap on a thin column down the side of the main feature. WHAT'S RIGHT ON AND WHAT'S RIGHT OFF.

'You see, I was influenced by the pictures of refugees I see on the television,' said Miranda. 'I was also influenced by those women I have observed recently, begging on the Tube.'

Lorna sighed. 'Miranda, don't you think that "Dying for Help" is a bit of a cliché? And also, who says these women are dying anyway? I mean, do you actually know?'

Miranda looked sullenly at Lorna. 'I don't see why I should have to write the headlines anyway,' she said. 'I don't really think I should have to spend so much time getting bogged down in the words.'

Lorna's phone rang; she picked it up to cover her confusion. 'Hi, it's me,' said Robin Moody. 'I'm sorry, who are you?' she said, annoyed. 'Oh look, I'm sorry, Robin, can't talk now,

I'm a little tied up here, for the moment,' she said, putting the phone down, but hoping her sudden change of tone might lend her a mystique. She looked round to check that Miranda had noticed. She was sorry to see, however, that Miranda had walked away.

She launched her email; INSUFFICIENT MEMORY, her computer flickered. CLOSE DOWN OTHER WINDOWS, it said. Lorna's temper flipped from tense to more tense. She tried again to get into the email; for the merest millisecond, something completely different flicked up on her screen. She saw arrows, a white square, a light bulb, rank upon rank of magic numbers. They disappeared and the screen just froze.

She noticed Beatrice, on the other side of the office, going about her business in a new-looking pair of little embroidered mules. She had a sudden stab of hatred. What the hell was she doing here, at this silly paper, promoting ignorance, foolishness, envy; silly women buying silly shoes in silly shops? She jabbed about with her mouse: no, nothing, no purchase. The wheels rolled tinnily along her desk.

'For fuck's sake, what is this?' Julie was saying to Kelly. 'I'm sorry, Kells, but what is this all about? Hume and Derrida and Nietzsche: all that is is a bloody name-drop. You haven't followed the brief at all.'

Lorna saw Julie raise her arm and lower it deliberately, scribbling all over the printout with her thick black pen. She was on her feet and over there in a moment. 'I read it over first, Julie. I thought it was absolutely fine.'

Julie pretended she hadn't heard her. 'Look at this stuff, Kelly,' she said, jabbing at the paper with her pen. 'What's all that about, then? You aren't in the Philly Soc now, you know, Kells. You're going to have to do a bit better than that.' She did a deeply, personally affronted look for a long and pregnant moment. She heaved herself woundedly from her chair. 'And now, you've made me late for my fucking lunch appointment,' she muttered as she left.

Kelly, Lorna saw, was crying, and the tears had primed her annoying snuffle. All afternoon, she sat at her desk, looking tearful. Lorna actually changed the tilt on her computer terminal, so she wouldn't have to catch her eye.

At around five, five thirty, Julie came back from her lunch appointment, her breath sour and her eyes bleary, the bow on her pompadour drooping over her head. 'I bought this book,' she announced loudly, plunging her hands deep in a plastic carrier. '*The Little Book of Depression*. What sort of a fucking title for a book is that, I mean to say? Makes me feel depressed just looking at it, if you know what I mean. Fucking nightmare scenario, fucking nightmare, if you know what I mean.'

'So why did you buy it then?' said Daisy, her eyes wide and deliberately elfin.

'Had a feeling someone might want to read it,' said Julie. 'I wonder who? Who, I wonder, will be the lucky beneficiary of my bounteousness? Who's the crybaby round here?'

The girls watched, half laughing, as Julie turned with her carrier bags to Kelly. 'Something tells me you are not the happiest of bunnies,' she said, holding out the book. 'Oh, hang on a minute, though.' She fumbled in another bag, from the chemist. 'I got you some cheapo perfume while I was at it. Just put it on every morning and you'll make things much pleasanter for the rest of us, would you, there's a dear.' She dropped the book and the perfume on Kelly's lap, but Kelly did nothing with her hands to take them. The book and the little phial rolled off her legs to the floor.

'Gluttony, pride, lust, wrath, envy, avarice, depression. It's one of the seven deadly sins,' said Julie, pleased, to her audience. No one met her eye, though, and a sudden embarrassment flooded over her face. 'Accidie, *accidia*, sloth, depression,' she said, crossing her arms and turning and gliding away. Kelly looked around her, dumbfounded, then picked up the book and the cheapo perfume and ran after her in tears.

'Daisy,' Lorna said, 'were you watching what just happened?'

'He he he,' Daisy said.

'Miranda,' Lorna said, 'were you watching what just happened?'

'Personally I welcome confrontation,' said Miranda. 'It gives me a chance to delineate the experience I have to bring to bear on the situation. It allows me to explain why I have taken the decisions that I did.'

Without thinking, Lorna marched straight over to Beatrice's cubicle. 'That's right, Lorna, she said she wanted to see you,' Beatrice's dishy PA replied. The tousled head looked up from inside the glazed-off cubicle and Beatrice waved at Lorna, smiling. 'So I take it she knows what it's all about,' the dishy PA said.

'I'd imagine so,' said Lorna, without really thinking about it. Actually, Lorna didn't really know what it was all about herself.

Lorna hovered by the desk uneasily, waiting for Beatrice to offer her a seat. 'As you will have noticed,' she said, 'things have not been running smoothly –' Before she could finish, though, Beatrice cut in.

'I've decided to let Peter go,' she said. She looked so different close up, in her corner cubicle, with her handsome chair and bookshelves. Her legs flopped as she let herself lounge backwards. 'It isn't working, is it? The damned man is a bloody liability. So I've decided to fire him, as of now.'

Lorna looked at Beatrice. She was staring straight ahead, as though at Lorna, but she had made her eyes go blank.

'I'm replacing him with Julie, who, thankfully, is agreeable to taking on the role at such short notice. We can sit down together and work out a way of integrating Julie's present duties with your own. I don't think the department has been working anything like efficiently with Peter running it. I'm sure we can work things out an awful lot better this way.'

Lorna looked at Beatrice, horrified. She was met with a coldness that made her innards shrink.

'Why not me?' she said in a voice she could hear was a bit

pathetic. 'Peter said the job was mine if I wanted it. I work so hard out there.'

'I'm sorry, Lorna, if you are disappointed by my decision.' Sparks of disdain flew like metal shavings off Beatrice's lovely form. 'We all agree, your work is excellent, and we very much want you to go on doing it. We just think that Julie is more likely than you are to do what needs to be done.'

'So what needs to be done then, as you see it?'

'Well, if you have to ask, you're obviously not the person to do it, are you?' Curly little wires cut into Lorna's arms. 'But I work so hard, I'm sure I do,' she said at last, in a small voice. 'I know I work really hard.'

'Your work is fine, more than fine,' said Beatrice, with a thoughtful placing of a small, pale hand on her chin. 'But I can't see you as a boss, somehow. I just can't see you in that role.' She gazed out of the window, downriver, past the old docks to the gasworks on the other side of Greenwich. 'Of course, if you don't think you can work under Julie, it's a free labour market out there. Of course, we'd all be sorry if it came to that, Lorna. But of course, it's up to you.'

'So what does Peter say?' Lorna said, defeated.

'He understands the necessity. The organisation has other plans for him.'

'And what about the party? What are we supposed to do about the party?'

Beatrice stood up, dismissing her, with a shrug of her cashmere sweater. 'I simply don't have time to worry about parties, Lorna,' Beatrice said.

Lorna wandered back to her workstation. She was aware of Julie smirking in her direction, half hidden by Daisy, giggling into a tiny mobile phone. She saw the back of Miranda's smooth, long head. Lorna's mind was grinding like a mill without grain in it, with thoughts about deserving and social justice. 'But I really did deserve it,' she said to no one, then wished she hadn't. Being reduced to deserving is a terrible thing.

A figure loomed, over by the sports desk. Peter, surprisingly, had arrived. He was smiling, he was watching the match with his cronies on the television. Lorna looked over and caught his eye. He smiled, and Lorna realised that Beatrice had not yet got round to informing Peter that she had sacked him. She glanced round at Beatrice's adorable secretary, who made a camp face and stretched out his hands.

'Oh, Christ on a bloody scooter,' she heard Julie saying, somewhere from behind. 'He really is the most pathetic sight. Ring security, Daze, they might want to clear him from the building.'

Lorna leapt to her feet.

'My dear,' Peter said, puffing deeply and blowing smoke rings. Lorna had taken him out for a cup of coffee to the one place where smoking was permitted in the basement shopping mall. 'So now she's given my job to that gorgon? Bea always was a fluffy-headed goose.'

Lorna didn't understand it. Peter had just been sacked, crushed, humiliated. And yet, he was already sitting taller and straighter. The sweat was drying round his hairline. His briefcase was done up. He crossed his legs and stretched them out in front of him. Peter for some reason was looking good.

'I couldn't stay long anyway this afternoon,' Peter continued. 'I just popped in for a moment, really, to see how you were getting on. I'd better be off,' he said, rising, 'I've an appointment in a minute. Give me a ring on my mobile if anything comes up.'

When Lorna got back upstairs, Julie and Miranda were in a confab over Peter's desk. 'Righty-oh then, I'll leave it with you, Miss Madam,' said Julie, glancing at Lorna in an unreadable way. 'I'm in for a briefing with old Bea in a mo.'

'Well,' said Lorna, just to break the ensuing silence. 'No one had bothered to tell him what was happening, you know.' The vehemence that had sounded so fitting inside her head came out half-cock and rather whiny. She was going to have to try a good bit harder than that.

'It says here, "The Modern Age Ran for 200 Years Only, from 1789 to 1989",' said Miranda. 'Seventeen eighty-nine to 1989, for heaven's sake. I mean to say.'

'Well, yes, I can see it's a bit grandiose,' said Lorna. 'It's grandiose but it's quite striking, don't you think?'

'Why 1789 to 1989, though? Wouldn't it look better if we made it from 1790 to 1990 or something? Why not round it up to 1800 to 2000? Nothing much is going to happen, surely, in a couple of years?'

'But you know why he chose those years, don't you, Miranda?' Lorna glanced at her, and saw with a shock that she did not. 'From the French Revolution to the collapse of communism in Europe,' said Lorna. 'I would imagine that is what the writer means.'

Miranda looked tearful. 'Remembering dates is such a boysy, pub-quiz thing. It's all I can do, keeping the cards up to date in my filing system. I can't be expected to monitor everything else.'

'Your rotary filing system is an absolute joy,' said Lorna, truthfully. Poor Miranda, she noticed, could not help but glow. 'Maybe we should go out for a drink one evening, so we can talk these things through.'

'Oh Lorna, I'd love to, but you know what?' said Miranda. 'I have to go early, in fact, this afternoon. I have so much to do at the moment, you know, particularly with the party coming up. I am due at two events this evening, and two parties tomorrow. I've already run all this past Julie, Lorna, who agrees that the party has to be my priority for the moment. I really don't think this is a good time, Lorna, for you to get in the way of that.'

'By the way, Lorna,' said Beatrice, approaching. 'By the way, about this page. Please change it, would you, before you leave the office this evening. I can see that it's powerful, but it's a bit of a cliché, don't you think?'

She held aloft the refugees on the hillside. The women were still labouring across the rocky moorland. Evil birds were still fluttering down the side. The splash headline was still DYING FOR HELP. Vegetables with the power of motion, thought Lorna; vegetables with the power of motion, ready to be pecked.

Chapter Seven

'She told me she was Julie's deputy, de facto,' said Robin Moody, pulling on a trainer over thick socks. 'Julie's deputy, de facto, that's exactly the phrase she used, right enough, that Miranda. Julie's deputy, de facto. The girl is a prize mule.'

'Oh, I suppose she is just frustrated, isn't she,' said Lorna mildly, folding up the spare duvet and pushing the futon back on its frame. It all looked so peculiar, her table with a man at it, and a plate of the breakfast buns she had bought the day before on the off chance, along with orange juice from an actual carton and coffee made in a pot.

Robin's teeth tore at a raisin bagel. 'And did you see that guy who came to collect her? Jesus, what a loser. What is he, a consultant, an accountant, an investment banker of some sort. What a loser, right enough.'

'Yes, but you have to admit, she did us proud with that party. You have to admit, Rob, Miranda did us proud.'

Parties are something else, Lorna thought to herself in her peeling bathroom, flushing hard at the cistern then waiting on to flush again. They are like the masques or ballets they put in drama of the olden days, the plays within plays that counterpoint the main action going on in the frame. She thought back and saw that room again abstractly: the great arcs traced along the floor as guests worked their way from person to person, clump to clump, each on a route according to his or her little secret map. She saw the dominant curves of the party's stars, the important people, sweeping into the room and around it, nodding and smiling at supplicants on their way. She saw the short, stabbing pathways of the shyer, the nervous, the more tentative, edging towards the centre then quickly falling back to the sides.

'The way we glide in and out of people's lives these days,' thought Lorna, standing to one side and watching, devilish little bubbles breaking on the back of her throat. 'The way you glide in and out of people's lives these days, like castors on a track.'

The party went ahead because it had to, Peter or no Peter, and, for what it was worth or not worth, Miranda really had done it well. A friend in public relations helped her get the use of a newly refurbished bar-restaurant in a grand old bank building: 'not so far,' as she put it to enquirers, 'from, you know, the Savoy'. The exterior was of Portland stone with scrolls and pilasters. The interior was all pale wood and chrome effect. The bar shone with metal and glass and ice and liquids. A great lantern hung from the ceiling, angular and prismatic, shattering the light.

'Well, Miranda, I think you've done us proud with this party,' Lorna said when she and Miranda, Julie and Daisy met up to discuss last-minute arrangements an hour before the party was due to start. In theory, Kelly should have been at that meeting also, but in practice, she was not.

'The task made full use, I felt, of my organisational acumen,' said Miranda, beaming.

'Would you say it was organisational acumen?' asked Lorna, with the precision she had been cultivating recently. 'Would you not say it was more like organisational flair?'

The girls stood around, pretending they liked each other, and what with the chrome, the pale wood, the party outfits, for a moment, they almost did. Miranda, good as her word, was wearing her black trouser suit dressed up with fuchsia-pink sandals and a matching pink pashmina. She had a new clipboard with her, fuchsia pink also, with a colour-coded guest list, and a silver pen. Julie was resplendent in old maroon crêpe velvet, with a pattern on it of huge man-eating flowers. Her pompadour was triumphal, and had a small net pinned to the front of it. Her mouth was extremely red. Her colours clashed unpleasantly with Lorna's aggressively plain grey skirt and saxe-blue jumper. Wasting and besting, sacrifice and destruction: it never does to forget how much a decent party has to do with hate.

'I've devised us a rota of our duties,' said Miranda, flipping through the papers on her clipboard. 'I thought we could take it in turns to greet guests and introduce them to people, and check them off on my list.'

'Apart from you, surely,' said Lorna kindly. 'We don't want to waste your organisational acumen by bogging you down at the door.'

'Big names, look, I've done in bold type, with a star ratings system. Please alert me, Daisy, as soon as any of these arrive.'

Daisy sat herself down at the front desk for the first shift, whooping as she read through the names on Miranda's list. She was wearing a puckish garment, like underwear, but with an artfully uneven hem. On her feet she had a pair of moon boots. She still wore her office earpiece round her neck.

'You look particularly cybernetic this evening,' said Lorna.

'Yeah, fine, whatever,' said Daisy, looking hurt.

A woman arrived, extremely pregnant, in an old brown evening cape. She looked around her, puzzled. No one came forward to help. She paused thoughtfully by a modern artwork. Miranda stood behind Daisy with her clipboard, engrossed in giving her a last-minute briefing. This is one good thing about hosting a party though, thought Lorna, watching without moving forward. Whatever else, at least you're not an interloper. At least you know that you belong.

Another of Miranda's contacts worked in the marketing department of a champagne vintner at that time eager to boost its profile among the city's latest new elite. More usually, it sponsored arts events and fashion shows, except that Miranda had persuaded them to sponsor the brainy-section party too. The contact was impressed with the talent on display in the guest list Miranda sent through for the vintner's approval; cleverly, she sent them her wish list rather than the actual RSVPs. The vintner proved remarkably generous. The first few bottles were really very good.

It was dry and golden, with streams of tiny bubbles. It was the taste of the city, of white lights and yellow lights strung like diamonds across great buildings of porous stone. Envy and anxiety ran round the room like electricity. Lorna set about drinking as much of the stuff as she could.

The party had gone ahead because it had to, Peter or no Peter, and anyway, as it happened, Peter was very much there.

Lorna phoned him up a couple of days beforehand, to see what he wanted to do. 'It's the party on Wednesday,' she said into his home machine, worrying she was being an intruder on private grief. 'I don't know if you remember, or what you want to do about it. I just thought you ought to know.'

'My dear, of course I know that it's the party,' Peter picked up the phone and broke in. 'And, well, of course I'll be there. Beatrice and I have talked it over. I think I'll give a little speech.'

'Really? You don't feel a bit weird about it?'

'No, of course not, why on earth should I? Bea and I, you know, you know what we're like. We're always on the best of terms.'

Lorna felt wrong and low and a little sour-smelling, like a weed in a formal garden. 'Great,' she said uncertainly. 'We'll all look forward to seeing you there. Do you want to meet up some- where beforehand? You know, for moral support?'

'Oh Lorna, that is so, so sweet of you,' Peter said, still in his public voice, as if he thought that someone was listening in.

He turned up, in his usual clothes, about an hour after the party started, just as the room was beginning to fill up. Peter,

Lorna saw, came into his own at a party. His gestures no longer looked too big for the space they had to fit in. His tie sat convivially on his chest. 'So yes, I decided to take a bit of a step sideways,' she heard him say to the mighty architect, a slight man with a stern expression, dressed in a tremendously black suit. 'You know, I'm in my element in a ceremonial role. Old Bea said to me, hey, Peter, you're just the guy for a bit of speechifying, just don't quote them too much of your dreary poetry. Oh, you know what she's like, good old Bea.'

It would make a fine scenario for a musical, thought Lorna, standing on her own. It could be one of those all-singing, all-dancing numbers, the girls in leotards, scissoring unkindly across the smooth pale floor. What a pity we won't have dancing later, like Tolstoy, like Jane Austen. What a pity we don't have that excuse.

'My dear!' said Peter, smiling widely and placing a hand upon her shoulder. 'You've been such an angel, such a trouper, such a wonder. You know.'

Lorna smiled and waited to be introduced to the mighty architect, and to the august lady now standing at his side. She never was, though. She never was. Peter wasn't really praising her or thanking her. He was making up to the chap by showing him that he, Peter, must be quite a fellow to inspire such loyalty from his elves.

'You really have been quite marvellous,' said Peter, smiling widely, his words beginning to slip out of sync with his expression, in the way they had so often done at work. The mighty architect wandered off with the august lady. Peter himself made ready to move on.

The party was just peaking as Beatrice arrived, flanked by her usual men. She was wearing a velvet frock coat, and shoes with witty flared heels, and her golden curly hair had been marcelled. Beatrice walked the room with deliberation, an assistant on either side of her, yoked like panniers to her shoulders. She was absolute power in this statelet. She was the sun.

Lorna watched Peter's eyes with interest. They were

following Beatrice, with such anxiety in them. She herself felt very small and suddenly annoying, tugging at the bottom of his jacket. He turned to look down at her, spluttering. He could hardly bear it. He so much wanted to be watching his old Bea.

The pregnant woman in the old brown evening cape was trying to catch her attention. Lorna did recognise her, sort of, but decided to avoid her eye. She felt guilty as she did it, but she made herself feel better by pretending she wasn't really doing what she was doing. She was short-sighted, she was terribly busy. She wasn't causing in another that dreadful shrivelling feeling she might feel if she caught someone doing this to her.

'Lorna, dear comrade!' The pregnant woman, undaunted, approached. 'I've been worried, I haven't heard from you for ages . . . Just reassure me, everything's all right . . .' She was red-cheeked and sturdy-looking, with gashed lines and a stoic cheerfulness. She had an old-fashioned upper-class accent. Oh for heaven's sake, Lorna thought.

'I just heard about Peter-chops,' the woman said. 'The running dog felled by inner contradiction . . . Don't you think?'

'I'm sorry?' Lorna's ears perked up.

'Oh, you know what I mean,' the woman said, with a warning look to the side. 'We'll talk about it later. This is not the time or place.'

Miranda marched up, beaming joyfully, her face shiny with exertion, her hand thrusting straight past Lorna's face. 'Hi there, Harriet, I'm Miranda, at last we meet, at last. It's such a thrill for me, I am such an admirer. It's the greatest pleasure to meet you.'

'But my dear girl, we met last week too, at that drinks thing . . . don't you remember?' Miranda's gay smile fell. 'I'm terribly sorry,' she said, on the back foot. 'I can't quite recall which one.'

The woman turned to Lorna with a practised rudeness,

blocking out Miranda with her bump. 'Actually,' she confided, 'that's a total porky, I didn't really . . . But you know, Lorna, I rather have the idea I don't want to be, what do you think?' She giggled in a way both lovable and demonic. Lorna noticed that she wore the same scent as Lady Bea.

'If you're that bothered about my state of mind why are you always flaking on our dates?' she asked.

'Oh Lorna, you know how it is, when you have a job and two small children. But we must definitely do something soon . . . Oh look, my phone's buzzing, I'll have to take it, it's probably the nanny . . . I'll catch you in a minute, Lorna. Hi, nanny, sorry, nanny, hi, Ruth.'

Lorna knew she was feeling anxious, a little empty, but she couldn't quite remember why. Then she saw him, arriving. He had another, smaller man at his side. Robin swept up and kissed her charmingly. The youngster walked away. Lorna thought Robin's eyes were a little glassy-looking. He was still wearing his usual trainers, but his suit was unexpectedly fine.

She poked him in a friendly way and said, 'Great suit, that, Robin.' She thought of saying, but didn't: 'You look like a proper media cock.'

'A man gave it me,' Robin said. His eye wandered to the surface of her cheek then bounced right off it. His eyes were simply not connecting. 'Are you high in some way?' Lorna asked.

'The thing about drugs is you mustn't let them confine you. Or define you indeed,' said Robin quickly, as though the remark were rehearsed.

Lorna looked at him ironically, raising her eyebrows.

'No, I'm no a druggie, Lorna,' said Robin, looking straight back at her with sadness in his eyes. 'If I may say so, that's a typically middle-class media-chick assumption to be making, about a guy like me.'

Lorna said she was sorry, and Robin shrugged. A girl came past with champagne flutes on a silver platter. 'Cheers, doll,' said

Robin. 'I'll catch you later, Lorna. Right now, I'd better go and find my pal.'

'And you yourself are looking lovely, right enough,' he said, with a look over his shoulder. 'I'll catch you later, I hope.'

She found herself ambushed by a group of women, younger than she, and even shorter. 'Daisy says you're awfully clever,' said the leader. She had bare arms and a top with sequins. 'What was your name again? What's your job? Do you like it? How did you get it? Do you get to see a lot of films?'

'I really wouldn't bother talking to me,' said Lorna. 'Try talking to those men over there. I'm not important enough, I've just been passed over for promotion. There's absolutely nothing I can do for you. Not that I would do it, even if I could.'

'La-di-da, will you look at Lady Beatrice,' said Robin. 'You should go and tell her you think she's marvellous.'

'But I don't, in all honesty. And I think she'd know.'

'Och, Lorna,' Robin said, cuffing her lightly on the arm. 'Who cares about in all honesty? This is no about all honesty, this is a party, right enough. One, they generally believe it, which makes it quite funny. And even if they don't believe you, they're pleased to see you try. It's like being a wee dog and offering your belly. It's saying, likesay, here you are.'

He dipped his head and made his eyes look up at her beseechingly. Lorna laughed and thrilled inside.

'Watch me, Lorna, watch me and mark.' And off he bounded, leaving Lorna on her own.

Beatrice, she was amazed to notice, looked delighted when Robin accosted her, taking her hand in his and kissing it lightly, with a satirical glance at Lorna and a mischievous bow. He went on holding her hand as they exchanged a few words after. She laughed and seemed to be pushing her chin in his direction. He said something she seemed to find especially funny, then he was back with Lorna, flushed.

'I didn't know you knew Lady Beatrice,' said Lorna.

'Oh, I've seen her, around and about.'

Lorna did not think she altogether trusted Robin Moody, but the thought, once thought, was forgot.

It was Lorna's turn for door duty when Beatrice and her minders made to leave. 'Goodnight, Beatrice,' Lorna called, 'Thank you for coming.'

'Goodnight, Lorna,' Beatrice called, as if she were the most enlightened monarch in the world. They were going on, Lorna supposed, to a more exclusive venue. Peter, she saw, was standing by with his ears flattened, hoping to get asked along.

'Oh, Lady Beatrice! She's so charismatic!' said someone standing near her. 'Such talent, in one so young!'

Lorna scanned the room again, ascertaining the current position of the others. Peter had retreated to a corner of the bar with the other tall men in tweedy jackets. He appeared to have forgotten all about his speech. Julie was standing with Sophie Pottinger from the smoking room, each at an angle to the other, showing off their finery, acting the grandes dames. She was drinking a diet cola, Lorna noticed. She wasn't going to spoil her night of triumph by getting drunk. Miranda was sitting at a table with Daisy and other youngsters. She was holding forth about something, and it seemed to be going down well. None of the big-name guests on Miranda's wish list had showed, though, apart from the mighty architect, now wandering about and looking lost and baleful on his own. It seemed a bit hard on Miranda, thought Lorna, going to all this trouble then having the party hijacked by all comers. The host puts all the work in and the guests make wheels within wheels.

'Want to smoke?' said Sophie Pottinger suddenly, sidling up to Lorna with a lit cigarette in her hand. It was not usual for Sophie Pottinger to offer cigarettes to the likes of Lorna; but then, it was not like Sophie Pottinger not to be wearing a stiff suit and scary spectacles, exchanged for the occasion with contact lenses and an ugly flounced dress. 'So Peter's gone, I hear, Julie's been telling me all about it. And now it seems that Bea herself is in the departure lounge.'

'I'm sorry?' said Lorna, feinting.

'I mean, she really is a bit of a joke, isn't she,' Sophie said, with her sly smile.

Lorna felt foolish, out of her depth. 'I'm sorry?' she said again.

'I don't know why you don't tell her to get stuffed, you know,' said Sophie Pottinger, leaning over the desk and talking sideways. Her dress was hideous, and terribly dear-looking. Lorna smiled again and pushed down.

'She says it's all your fault, obviously, but she would, really, wouldn't she?'

'I'm sorry,' Lorna said desperately. 'I must be terribly naive, I think. I really don't know what you mean.'

'Oh, I don't think you're naive,' Sophie Pottinger said, pouting. 'I think you know perfectly well what you're about.' A sneaky grin played round her mouth. Lorna looked again for Robin, but she couldn't see him anywhere. The thought of Sophie caused her to look around for Robin; but Robin, for the moment, was lost.

She did see Kelly, though, terribly late, and wearing the strangest outfit. 'There you are,' said Julie, wandering up, with Daisy, arm in arm. 'My, my, young Kelly. Whatever have you got on?' Her tight black skirt seemed to have elastic in it, making it both clingy and unwieldy. She was still wearing her old ankle boots, and they looked curiously chunky, stuck on the ends of her bandy legs. Her jumper was like a cheapo version of Lorna's and she had dyed her hair and curled it in a parody of Lady Beatrice. She looked lovely in her way, with her white skin and her bony sternum. She looked like a girl possessed by malignant spirits. She looked a bit like a wraith.

'You look lovely,' said Julie, laughing unkindly.

'You look lovely,' said Lorna, meaning well.

The mighty architect, it was said, was a recovering alcoholic. And there he was, under the shattered lantern, drinking, his first taste of spirits for more than seven years. You see these tragedies out of the corner of your eye. He had his steely hair and his stern face; the glass he was holding was fashionably bulbous. He looked like a distinguished man, just drinking. That was the end of his last chance, his seven-year sobriety. He would never manage it again.

'Peter Pevensey!' Harriet's eyes went to the ceiling. 'I am sure you don't need me to tell you. He would sell his grandmother for less . . . Watch him carefully, Lorna, especially now that he seems to be on a downer. Watch him like a hawk . . .'

'I quite like him,' said Lorna. 'I admire the way he refuses to let it all get him down.'

'Trust me on this,' said Harriet, sticking her bump out, 'I've been around this scene longer than anyone. I'm telling you, you can't trust any of them.'

'So why should I trust you?'

'Because it's like stepping stones. You can't manage by trusting no one. So you have to move quickly and hope for the best.'

'Actually,' Lorna said, 'I'm not entirely sure who you are, you know. I've lost my memory, I've had some sort of a brainstorm. Only, I haven't told anyone about it, I'm kind of scared to. I haven't a clue what I'm supposed to do next.'

'Yes, dear comrade, I wondered if that might be the trouble,' said the liberal scion, who evidently had not listened to a word. 'Well, look, we'll talk about it later, I have to go now, the nanny needs me . . . Look, I'll mail you, I'll give you a ring or something . . . We really must meet up.'

It was long past closing time; the party had entered the devastation stage. People were standing around with their legs locked, heavy coats against silk and light wool. Lorna caught a glimpse of Kelly, gluttonous for punishment, trying to talk to the mighty architect, drunk now and thoroughly disgruntled. Kelly was standing on tiptoe, the heels on her ankle boots poking out behind her. She was so drunk now, she could barely talk. The architect looked around him for an escape hatch. Lorna had a there-but-for-the-grace-of-God frisson.

'I'll be off then,' she said to no one, realising that she was more than a little tight herself. She grabbed her coat from the rack and stepped outside. The stone facing the portico was beautiful, its surface broken by tiny fossils and holes where shells had been. People in taxis were going north and east and westwards. 'I'm going south,' she wanted to say, brightly and pertinently. She was afraid to open her mouth.

Robin appeared from behind her somewhere and took her arm. 'Look, Lorna, look,' he said, 'all the bonnie wee fossils.' 'My hero,' Lorna said, and she really meant it. 'Bonnie wee fossils, right enough.'

'I'm no coming with you unless you ask me,' he said, giving her one of his intent looks. She thought she felt him bite her ear in the taxi but she wasn't sure. 'I'm no coming up the stairs unless you ask me,' he said, after he had paid the driver, giving vent to the divinest chuckle. Lorna kept her eyes and mouth shut and thought very hard about the futon she had for visitors rolled up under her bed.

'OK, so, those people in the lift,' said Robin, sitting at Lorna's trestle table with a pencil in his hand. 'They go down on the odds lift, all the way to the ground they go, they go up again on the evens one straight after. They go down, they go all the way up again, just to go one floor up.' He munched his way through the almond mini-croissant and the cinnamon Danish. He was eating her out of house and home.

The flat's whole ecosystem was altered with Robin in it. The main room looked messy and overcrowded with his jacket on the floor. Already her toilet smelt a new smell of delicious hormones. There were new crumbs on the floor under the seat where he was sitting and a new smear of toothpaste round the sink. Her teapot was cracked, Lorna noticed, a thin crack, all the way up one side; she turned it so the unbroken part faced outward, keeping the cracked bit to herself.

'Great library you have here, Lorna,' said Robin, stretching in his chair to examine the spines on the book-pile most close to where he sat. 'No what you'd expect of a thwarted operative on the very worst newspaper in the land.'

'A thwarted operative?' said Lorna. 'So I'm a thwarted operative now?'

'It's quite a cosy wee home you have here in general,' said Robin, stretching his body in his chair. 'Very cosy and, I think, very Lorna.'

'And what, pray, might "very Lorna" mean?'

'Well, it's no the most luxurious of the anchoress cells I've visited, if you get my meaning.'

'So you are in the habit of visiting many of these places? Are you saying you are a connoisseur?'

Robin laughed, and dug into his pocket for his shag tin. Lorna asked him if he wouldn't mind coming with her and taking his coffee outside. They folded up their chairs and carried them on to the little patio; there was now a leggy lavender Lorna had bought from the florist in the corner, and a scruffy ivy she was hoping to train over the crumbly bits in the sparkly tiles.

'The anchoress in her heavenly walled-up garden,' Robin said, then froze. 'Jesus, Mary and Joseph,' he said. 'That's asbestos, so it is, there. That's solid asbestos, right enough.' He was looking at the crumbly old cladding on the barrel-vaulted water tower. Neither stone nor wood nor metal nor plastic. The minute he said it, Lorna knew he was right.

'Of course I know about asbestos,' said Robin. 'I'm from the west of Scotland, right enough. My grandfather died of mesothelioma, did I no say that? He worked as a lagger on the ships. My granda died of bloody mesothelioma, a truly terrible death. It took them three days to get him cremated, he had so much of that poison in his body. That's a joke, by the way, Lorna, no the bit about the pain, but.' Lorna did not laugh.

Slowly, Robin licked his index finger and ran it down the mysterious surface, stroking the tiles gently along their grain. '"I study you glout and gloss, but have / No cadrans to adjust you with, and turn again / From optik to haptik and like a blind man run / My fingers over you, arris by arris, burr by burr,"' he said. 'MacDiarmid, you know, the big man MacDiarmid, the phase

after the Scottish phase, a poem called "On a Raised Beach".
Great stuff, MacDiarmid. My main man.'

Lorna watched the finger, entranced.

'I would say that is chrysotile, white asbestos, in a cement-
like compound,' said Robin gravely. 'It's not good, but it's no the
worst, which would be crocidolite, which is the blue. The stuff
seems stable enough, it's no giving off dust or fibres. Have a
word with the council about it and try not to touch it. Now, my
sweetness, I have to love you and leave you. I've got a morning
appointment. Not for the first time, his lips brushed against her
knuckles. 'That was a wonderful evening, right enough,' he said,
'with a most joyous and unexpected conclusion. Maybe we can
do something similar sometime. I'll be in touch, I'll be in touch.'

Lorna was swooning so much, she felt she might be having
another brainstorm. And maybe she did fall slightly, because then
she felt Robin's arm go around her. He chuckled gently, she gazed
up at his vicious jawline. A staircase rose from hell to heaven,
breaking the very crust of the earth.

Chapter Eight

Julie stuck her nodding dog on top of her computer, along with a horrid poppet and the leprosy tin. 'It's the triumph of the underdog,' she said. 'Isn't it, Wowser?' She picked up the dog and held it nodding in front of her. 'Yes it is, Mistress Julie,' Wowser said in a silly put-on voice. 'Cry havoc and let slip the underdogs of war,' said Julie, shaking the dog up and down. 'Wow wow wow,' said Wowser, wobbling. 'Wow wow wow.'

In some ways, Julie's promotion was a feelgood testament to fairness and social mobility. She was not a man and she didn't have influential backers; her surname was not a well-known one that brought a subliminal great-and-good glow to readers when they noticed it on a page. She just sat there and waited, and sat there waiting, and waited for her turn.

'I worked myself up from the bottom of the table,' Julie said, and she said it often. 'I started out as a humble gofer on a young people's pop-music magazine.

'I worked myself up from the bottom of the table. Unlike a public-schoolboy twit like that Pevensey moron, never did an honest day's work in his life.

'I worked myself up from the bottom of the table, and nobody ever helped me,' said Julie. 'She's such a fucking nightmare, that bloody woman. Doesn't she know that punctuality is of the essence round here?'

With Peter sacked and Julie promoted, the department was one person down. Beatrice pledged to fill the position, as soon as she got the go-ahead, but in the short term, this meant there was a lot more work for everyone to do. There was more work for everyone, including Kelly, who seemed eager to make a last-ditch attempt.

'Look, I got a purse just like your one,' she said to Lorna. 'They're really great, aren't they?'

'Well, they're only purses,' Lorna said, puzzled. 'I mean, they're fine for keeping money in, if that's the sort of thing you mean.'

'Yes, her performance is getting increasingly erratic,' Lorna heard Miranda say to Julie, a little later on. Miranda had moved desks to squat at Kelly's one, next to Julie, over the lunch hour; the two of them were sharing a tub of taramasalata and a bag of carrot sticks. These days, Lorna quite often came in to find Miranda sitting in Kelly's seat, in conversation with Julie, straining sideways. 'Not, I suppose, that she even has a best friend, fnur fnur,' she could hear Julie saying. 'Did I tell you, my dear, the company insists on giving me a mobile phone for free?'

Lorna sat down at her computer with a heavy heart. She felt a bit lost sometimes, with Peter's desk in front of her, empty, and Miranda's desk next to her, empty too. She launched her email browser, hoping that Harriet, for once, might have answered one of her messages. No Harriet, even. Harriet seemed to have disappeared.

Miranda's phone went, so Lorna picked it up. 'Miranda isn't at her desk at the moment,' she said to the person at the other end. 'Look, Miranda, I've got my own work to do,' she rattily snapped straight after. 'Why don't you swap desks properly if you want to sit over there?' 'That won't be necessary, Lorna,' Miranda said smoothly. 'Julie and I will finish our meeting shortly. Just leave my phone on voicemail, Lorna, if you find you're getting stressed.'

That night, Lorna woke up to find herself shrieking and weeping, with Robin Moody standing over her in his shorts and T-shirt, rubbing her back. She had been thrashing at her pillow, apparently. She had been fighting it to the death. 'Lassie, lassie,' said Robin, 'is it really that bad? Did you really want that silly job that much?' Yes she had, was the truth of it, but she wasn't going to say that to Robin Moody. 'I don't know what all that was about,' she mumbled, and pretended to go back to sleep.

A fever broke that night, and after it, Lorna found herself calmed down. 'We had better have lunch, hadn't we, you and me,' she said to Julie, having taken a deep breath first. 'All right,' said Julie, looking hounded. Come lunchtime, Lorna watched her sneak off on her own, not returning to the office until the back of four.

In so many ways, Julie was a marvellous person, that was the difficult thing. She shone with brains. Her observations were acute, often. She could be very, very funny. She would have made a marvellous stand-up comedian or chat-show hostess. Also, Julie had been at the paper for as long as anyone could remember, through all manner of tribulation. Through all manner of crisis and upheaval, she had stuck it out and clung on. She had clung on and she had taken legendarily good care of Daisy, interjecting herself bodily, it was said, when some past bogeyman had attempted to bawl her out. Lorna had no recollection of this incident, what with her isolation and her brainstorm. It always seemed mysterious to her, and a pity, the strength and uncon-ditionality of Julie and Daisy's bond.

'I'll give you a thump, I will,' said Julie one day, when Daisy had messed up the page she was doing.

'He he he,' was Daisy's tinkling reply.

'Come the day of the glorious revolution, I know who'll be first up against that wall of shelving.'

'He he he,' said Daisy. 'He he he.'

'Bring in sharia law, that's what I say. Then we can just cut their bloody hands off and that would be the end of the whole thing.'

'She's a bit salt of the earth, isn't she?' the gimlet-eyed Sophie Pottinger said to Lorna by the photocopier one day. 'Not at all the sort of person you'd expect to find in a job like that, but she's simply splendid, salt of the earth.'

Except that Julie wasn't really what Sophie meant by salt of the earth at all, and that she appeared so was only because the world of business can be so crazy, with its prejudice, its superstitions, its magical belief in the power of certain names. Julie's father owned a chain of garages and her mother was a beauty therapist, and they had sent their girl to a private day school for young ladies near Bristol, which was where they lived. 'School for young ladies?' Julie would say when telling anecdotes of her schooldays. 'More like school for bloody elves. They were titchy, all of them, with legs like bloody sparrows. Legs like bloody sparrows, they had, in their little white socks.

'But lumps do rise to the top, my poppets,' Julie continued. And it was at the school for young ladies that she first discovered this truth. She was extremely tall for her age then and had a fruity laugh on her, and if she laughed loud enough, she noticed, she could make everyone else join in. She made special friends with small girls, whom she liked to squash in angular bear hugs. They went on shoplifting trips to the city centre, and thence to Chinese restaurants for enormous meals. It isn't hard for a woman to get what she needs through browbeating and intimidation: most people don't know what they want, really, out of situations, and are perfectly happy for you to tell them what to do.

She had a special knack with the student feminists of the 1980s, with their mad masochistic politics of woman-centred non-violence and sisters under the skin. If ever anyone disagreed with her in meetings, she skilfully prompted them to consider how bad they felt about themselves instead. She talked in lewd detail about sexual matters, implying that the others might be puritanical and hung up. She exaggerated her West Country accent when the discussion turned to social class. If a sister was getting too pleased with herself or something, Julie just stared at her, letting her eyes cross and her chin go double. The sister would falter and go silent, realising how shallow she was, how unsisterly, how vain. Most of them had eating disorders anyway, so were already weakened, being most of the time half starved.

She also found it easy on the pop-music paper where she got a job straight after, as secretary to the record-reviews section and the letters page. It was the middle 1980s, the much-misunderstood angry-pop-group era. Rows flamed across the pages of Julie's paper, about meat-eating, Northern Ireland, the miners, whether it was possible or otherwise for pop music to be usefully left-wing. Even the letters page hectored the readers, with little mocking footnotes added to the ends of their laborious communications. 'How can you possibly compare the awesome talents of the bog-eyed heart-strummer Costello to the prancing theatric posturing and gutless soul-less whine of Bowie? Maybe because you are stupid,' went one. 'Have you ever considered that the reason your letters get cut is because they are so whiningly self-righteous and BORING?' was how another began. Julie turned out to have a great talent for this sort of thing: 'What you smirking bourgeois veg-fascists fail to realise is the importance of dead-animal flinging to working-class culture,' was how she started her first attempt. 'Lovely stuff, Jules,' said the letters-page editor, a quiet boy with a constant tremor. 'Lovely stuff, Jules. Do some more sometime.'

At first, the journalists felt sorry for poor Julie, so tall and shy and stooping, with the thick hair she dyed dead black at that time and wore across her face. They felt sorry for her, but also, they found her cosy. These underfed goblins had come to London too soon really, too soon for them to last. Their jobs exposed them to impossible amounts of noise, disturbance, corruption. They lived on record-company freebies, record-company sandwiches, record-company snorts and lines. They were in a constant state of fatigue and aggravation, and it made them desperate for affection. Julie watched these misguided people take pity on her, trying not to discriminate against the lanky girl with the long black hair. She was always on hand for a bony cuddle when cuddles were needed: there is nothing a weak person likes better than a chance to nestle for a moment in the lee of the strong.

Nice people are weak people, especially those eighties trendy lefties, with their easy dole money and their student grants. They are used to having things just given to them, which makes them sloppy, not good at seizing things for themselves. And as for public-schoolboy idiots of the Pevensey-type boss class, they're so used to just getting things given to them, the whole of life is just one big freebie. It's not as if they even need their jobs in the first place, do they? It's not as if they even need to work.

And there's another thing about these nice, weak people. They can bear to have things taken away from them; it's never quite the end of the world. They are philosophical about it. They assume there will be more where the first one came from. They can just work harder, learn their lessons, be more careful next time. Whereas, thought Julie, if anyone so much as touched her forties collection, her heart would break like aged Bakelite on a flagstone floor. Her deco armchair, her walnut wireless, her flowered tea dress, her 78s: most of the money she made from the charity tin and her other ventures went straight into building up her collection. She loved spending evenings at her fireside, drinking hot toddies and eating thin-cut bread and butter, with a crooner on the gramophone, while above her and around her wagged the searchlights and wailed the sirens; and far off, around her office in the Docklands, could be heard the crashing, bursting sound of bombs.

*　　*　　*

110

Lorna knew she shouldn't let it happen, but her skills were beginning to run in reverse. Instead of getting better with practice, her work was getting worse and worse. 'A grizzly mess,' an author wrote on her pages, unchallenged. 'D***** C****' – a famous actor – 'was totally unphased.' 'The enigma is intriguing and beguiling,' Miranda wrote in an intro. Lorna let it stand. She even left a rogue apostrophe on a big splash headline; she simply didn't see it until the page came back from Beatrice, the error ringed in red. Any week now, she expected a massive mistake on the pages, like a cigarette burn in a nylon stocking; only so far, it hadn't happened. Every week, though, Lorna could tell she was reading less and less of the brainy section, and with less and less attention. Every week, Lorna could tell she was doing less and less proper work.

But to begin with, Lorna was quite happy really, her attention absorbed by her affair with Robin Moody. Two or three times a week, along he came to her flat with a change of underwear in a football holdall, and a bag of groceries that he cooked on Lorna's black and filthy stove. He made squid-ink risotto and tortellini in *brodo*. He brought salads composed of unheard-of leaves and stalks. When Lorna made him her Scotch broth with leeks and barley once he laughed and said Scotland was no longer like that. But the dish could be easily updated with a chiffonade of parsley and a squirt of truffle oil.

After they had eaten, they would go out walking, wandering late at night across the parkland and the nearby streets. It was much easier with Robin there, dancing down footlit paths and round by the lock-up garages. Once, he sat down at her rickety table and mended the toadlike computer. It came back to life quite easily, but with its hard disk wiped. Another time, they sat among the harsh and looming asbestos tiling, with the pot of leggy lavender and glasses of red wine. 'What I don't understand is, what comes before alienation?' Lorna asked, still working her way through Hegel's *Phenomenology*. 'That's an ahistorical question, I think you'll find, my bonnie wee Lorna,' Robin said, chuckling, cuffing her gently on the head. The city lay below them in tilting compositions along the river: Millbank, the Shell Centre, the NatWest Tower, Guy's. Robin dipped his fingers in his shag tin and rolled them each a cigarette.

One evening, they were clattering back through the undertow and into the downstairs lobby when they met the epaulettes couple, making their way out of the evens lift. Lorna looked at Robin skywards, and he grinned. 'Good evening,' he said, with his gregarious west of Scotland accent. 'I hope you'll no mind us asking, but we've often seen you here about these parts. Why do you come down the one side and up the other side on the lifts like that?'

'Saves walking up the stairs, innit,' the woman said, looking at the floor. 'Joseph here, he's got back pain, and chest pain, and leg pain. Joseph here, he is not at all a well man.'

Robin clucked at her gently with his tongue. 'The shopping and that must be hard, right enough. Tell me the number of your flat and that, and I'll come in past on Saturday and see if you need a wee hand.'

'You shouldn't say these things unless you mean them,' said Lorna.

'Of course I mean it,' Robin said. But then, the coming Saturday happened and Robin appeared to forget. Lorna remembered but she said nothing. She didn't want to do shopping for her neighbours. She wanted her day with her lovely Robin all to herself.

Saturday turned to Sunday: they went out to the minimart on the corner to buy the papers then sat at Lorna's trestle table, drinking tea from Lorna's dangerous cracked teapot and eating wedges of lightly leavened cake. Peter, though sacked, was still writing his silly column, and had started using it to reflect on the disappointments and ironies of his youth. 'For heaven's sake, Lorna, when will we ever get enough of it?' said Robin. 'Art, science, socialism, religion. Nothing would ever get done for any of them if everybody just wanked on and on about their fucking dreary childhoods all the time.'

Art, science, socialism, religion, thought Lorna. That a man of such a fine austerity can also be bothered with the cooking and eating of rich food.

'I mean, this is the problem with that work you do on that fucking terrible comic,' Robin was saying, as he often said. 'It's no real writing, it's no real thinking, it's no part of the real movement of the world. You should know better, Lorna, you with all your lovely books.'

Robin said he was working hard on an idea of his for something creative, my creative writing project, he said. Lorna felt wistful when he mentioned it, like part of herself was lost and drifting on those long, long evenings when Robin was out of touch. She didn't see him for days on end sometimes. He was staying in, he said, at his house-sit, working on his project, day and night. She would come round, she said, she would bring him some food or something; but he didn't want it. He said the house-sit was horrible and filthy and squalid. He said it made him feel ashamed. Lorna considered just visiting him anyway, mainly to spy on him; then she realised he had been careful never to mention his house-sit's address.

'I don't know what goes on in that head of yours, Lorna,' he would say, ruffling her hairdo. 'I have absolutely no idea.'

One night, as Lorna was coming home late from a long, long day at the office, she saw her building bright with floodlights, with people crowded round the foot of it and officials in yellow tabards running about. Birds were tweeting, poor creatures, confused by the lighting. Lorna started to run. Her first idea was that the police had 'got' Robin, though for what they would have 'got' him exactly, she could not have said. Her second idea was that he had thrown himself off the building, and that somehow, it was all completely her fault.

When she got closer, though, she saw the beloved face of Robin himself, under the hood of his old dark parka, waving at her from the crowd. A publicity-seeker, a woman, was abseiling down the tower block; a TV crew was filming it for posterity. She was the first woman in the world to abseil down such a tall

113

domestic building. A researcher from the *Guinness Book of Records* was at hand. Lorna hugged Robin under his parka, and for the first time ever, she felt she really meant it. She was longing for the day Miranda would say to her, 'Robin Moody called again.' She would say, 'Oh, Robin,' and Miranda would say, 'Is he your boyfriend?' 'Of course he's my boyfriend,' Lorna would say; 'didn't you know that?' and Miranda would remember him from the night of the party when he looked so handsome, and perhaps she would take note.

The trouble was, she thought, the next day at the office, these long nights made her so terribly tired in the mornings, tired and apathetic and desperate to be in bed. She started skipping her breakfast porridge and buying Danish pastries, and card-board cups of coffee from the franchise in the mall. She ate egg-mayo sandwiches because they were the softest, and muffins, and chocolate brownies. Tiredness made her feel more than ever that she was slipping cogs and missing something, seeing what was important about a situation only after it was already over, like from the wrong end of a telescope, out of the corner of her eye.

'Robin, Robin, Rab Moody, yes, of course, I know him, of old,' Julie was saying down her receiver. 'Bit of a fucking tosser, but yes, I suppose, quite bright.'

Lorna's ears flipped flush to the side of her head.

'Had lunch with him myself the other day,' she continued. 'That's right, you know the one. No, it's not in our paper, fuck me, we can't afford him, can we. It's in the snooty one, start out as you mean to go on and all that. I'm sure he'll go far, that boy, up somebody's arse if not his own one. Up somebody's arse if not his own one. Fnur fnur fnur.'

Lorna flipped through back copies of the snooty paper. When she got to page 9 or 13 or 11, her horror was too big for her mouth. There was a generic picture of a council estate in the rain, and another of Robin, looking soulful. There was a label: ESTATE OF THE NATION: OUT AND ABOUT IN UNDERCLASS BRITAIN.

There was a credit line: By Robin Moody. And this is how it went:

> LIFE'S TOUGH for everybody these days, but for Joey, our downstairs neighbour, it's just got tougher still. I run into him in the lobby, waiting by the lifts: can't manage them stairs no more, mate, he says . . .

She grabbed her cigarettes and made for the smoking room. Her armpits were stinking. She read on:

> And what would I do, mate, he asks me, without my Mel here? Melanie is Joey's girlfriend, fatter even than he is, but more together, somehow. His other half, his better, his best mate ever, he calls her. His good girl, his lady, his tower of strength . . .

'"His good girl, his lady, his best mate ever",' thought Lorna. 'This is awful stuff, awful, awful. How dare he, the evil sneak?'

She returned to her desk and started writing Robin an email. 'You hypocrite,' she tapped, 'you horrible hypocrite. You are making my neighbours look foolish for no useful purpose. You are making money out of other people's pain.'

But she hadn't finished the column, unfortunately. So she stopped writing and read on. The narrative flipped, within a couple of paragraphs, away from Lorna's neighbours and back to something Robin probably did know an awful lot about:

> Even when the sheets of scarring were covering his lungs, my granda would have baulked to take a lift instead of a single flight of stairs . . .

Such a hideous word, 'baulked', thought Lorna, so redolent of the phoney. But at least the poor man was dead, and hopefully, not looking down.

The telly was on to a daytime confessional: the accusations, the showdowns, the self-pity and self-absorption, the constant proclamation of me-me-me. Oh Joey, oh Mel, oh Trisha, oh humanity.

'"Oh Joey, oh Mel, oh Trisha, oh humanity,"' Lorna thought. 'Indeed.' She stabbed at her phone with Robin's number; he didn't pick it up.

'Hello, it's me, Lorna,' she said in a clipped voice. 'It's four thirty. Please phone me back right away.'

Except that he didn't, and nor did he answer when she called him again at four forty-five.

Lorna spent the rest of the afternoon writing email after email. Her feelings were packed and painful, and their emphasis kept changing. She found it difficult to pick out the words.

'It is invasive and pornographic,' went one email. 'You make people look ugly and stupid, but the really ugly, stupid thing is your awful writing.'

'Your grandfather would be horrified,' went another. 'You're an emotional carpetbagger and a leech.'

'Endless self-pity and self-absorption? Well, it takes one to know one, right enough.'

She stayed on in the office until late that evening, calling him every hour. At last, at 10 p.m., he answered. 'I think you're just jealous, Lorna,' he said after a moment, sounding thoughtful, 'because you're wasting away in that job of yours, instead of doing something more creative and getting on.'

'You never even went in to visit, like you said you would,' said Lorna.

'I did so. I dropped in past, I offered to help them with her messages. We had a chat, like I put down. More than you've ever thought of doing for any of your neighbours, Lorna. Never mind all that talk about wanting to be part of something bigger than yourself.'

'But she's my fucking neighbour, not yours,' Lorna wanted to say, but even to her that sounded petulant, so she held it back.

116

'So you'll be going round to your pal, will you,' she said eventually, 'to show her what you've been writing?'

'Of course I will,' Robin said. 'Me and Melanie and Joseph, we're like that.'

'Well, don't bother coming in past me, then, will you,' she said, still wishing the opposite in a way. 'Don't bother coming in past me ever again.'

'Och, Lorna, if that's the way you want it,' said Robin sadly; 'but it's a terrible shame, right enough. I'll give you a ring when I come next to visit Mel and that. If you don't want to see me, you don't have to, but I'll give you a wee ring.'

'You were only after what you could get from me, weren't you?' said Lorna bitterly, as she put down the phone. But isn't that always true of relationships? she was thinking. Wasn't that just as true of her as well?

On her way home, on the way out of the tube station, Lorna was so overcome with anger that she took a coin out of her handbag and phoned him up again.

'But how the hell could you do it, Robin? You must have known it would piss me off.'

In the silence that followed, she eventually got it. Robin really didn't care. 'The trouble with you, Lorna,' he said at last, 'is you're no quite honest with yourself about what you want. Like all the rest of us, you want love and power in some configuration, and like all the rest of us, you've to decide what you will do and will no do in order to get it. I give you that piece of advice for nothing, right enough, and I would ask you please to think it through. I'm turning my phone off now and I'm getting the number changed tomorrow morning. Please don't bother to phone me again.'

In her flat, she sat herself hunched in a huddle by the radiator then realised she had completely run out of cigarettes. A drum-and-bass riff came up the heating pipe; she thought about running down the fire escape and throwing herself on the mercy of this party, but she found that she was too scared. She was too scared, too worn, too pathetic, really. She was beating off fear and tiredness, with weakening pigeon wings.

117

She went through the bin bag in the kitchen, searching it for butt ends. She found some, soaked, under coffee grounds and vegetable parings. She went through lint and fluff at the bottoms of her pockets. She picked single strands of tobacco from little cracks in her floor. Between the various sources, there was just enough for one roll-up. It tasted toxic, of melting plastic, but she smoked it for the three puffs it had left.

That night, there was a real storm, and the wind blew round and round the flat. The waste pipes gurgled like waterfalls. She lay in bed staring drily at the yellow light on the landing. At about 3 a.m. someone came and banged on her door, shouting. It wasn't Robin, there was more than one of them. After what seemed like a terribly long time they got fed up and went away.

Her door shook and rattled in its badly fitting frame. The lift clanked and thumped like manacles. Far, far below, she heard carousing, and alarm bells. 'I should have heard them far, far sooner,' she thought drowsily, on the verge of waking. 'I should have heard them far, far, sooner,' she thought on the verge of consciousness without ever entirely waking up.

The next morning, the weather had blown itself out. Her flower-pots were all knocked over. The water was pooling in the disappointing bulge in the tiles. A gurgle of blessedness rose again in her gorge, and something elsc. It took her a while, and then she got it. At long last and in spite of her brainstorm, Lorna was beginning to go sane.

She ran all twenty floors down the fire escape, and the views were staggering, cubes and cuboids and solid wedges, every housing type imaginable at all angles, slanting further and further as you got lower and lower, floor by floor and step by step. She ran right up them again, and she was there, flat out. She had her bath, she got dressed and she ran again, to the station. An idea popped into her head from nowhere. She was going to get fit.

Chapter Nine

Now that she wasn't smoking, Lorna's body was riddled with holes and twinges. The smoke, she realised, had been covering the holes up, deadening her nerve ends, and without it, her body teemed with little worries that rose, like streams of bubbles, then went pop at the top. At first, Lorna tried to follow the fizzing movements, back to source, forward to eventual outcomes. But they went nowhere in particular, they were in random motion. It was up to Lorna to impose some order on them, so she started to run.

She started slowly, like a joke person, in an old vest and baggy trousers. She could not believe it was possible to run so slowly. She seemed to move more slowly, even, than she would have done standing still. She ran so slowly, and yet she passed by people who were walking. It was as though they were being propelled backwards and she was running on the spot. To begin with, she ran in a curly line, from the bottom of her tower and round by the branch library on the precinct. It was like dragging her own dead body, round and round. She was pushing herself against nothingness, her own nothingness and failure. She was pushing herself in a knot through the middle of her heart.

As she ran, she breathed more slowly and more slowly.

Sometimes for long moments she didn't even breathe at all, and then when she did breathe, it was impossibly slow and sad. She ran past bin bags, bits of burger, smears of milk and dog-dirt. She smelt diesel bus-breath, high and rotten, rotten death smells, rotten death. Sometimes there was a spike of herbs in there, crushed by Lorna in the act of running. Cigarettes and reefer smoke came and went in clouds.

By night, if she had been working late at the office, she ran on the side of the main road. There was a trick to passing people wide, on the outside of the pavement, so they would have no worries that you were going to attack. She ran on the spot at kerbsides, waiting for gaps in the traffic. She crossed a side street, dodging jammed-up cars. She caught the eye of a man seated high in his delivery van, in his duct-taped wing mirror. The backs of her legs were like the cables that hold up bridges. Little fins of muscle were growing up her sides.

A boy outside the tube station picked up a cigarette butt from the pavement and stuck it in his mouth. A girl came out of the station, cracking open her phone. The boy snibbed the butt and started following, in the shadows of parked cars; the girl was oblivious, chattering to her pal. Lorna tailed them, fearless in her trainers, turning off where they did into a street of tall, blank houses and low-slung silver cars. The boy was closing in on the girl now. 'Excuse me, miss!' Lorna shouted. 'Excuse me, miss, over here!' The young man jerked and changed his course of action. The girl was safe, still phoning. Lorna sprang off on her way.

Julie made a periwig for Wowser out of a scrap of the office carpet; this was her current running joke. 'Sir,' she said. 'Like a woman on hind legs, sir! Like a woman on hind legs! Sir! As the good Sam Johnson would say!'

Miranda looked panicky. 'Who is Sam Johnson? Is he that actor in that play?'

Things were not going well at the paper. A memo went round on the email ordering everyone to label their desks and computers and put all their things into plastic crates. When they arrived back in the office on the Monday, the desks were configured exactly as they had been, except that they were all now a little closer crammed. The south-western section, with the lovely view of the river running down past Greenwich, had been partitioned off and was standing empty, apart from a pinky-lilac plush-covered podium and a foldaway projection screen. A management consultant was moving in to observe them, Sophie Pottinger told Lorna. 'You know what that means,' she darkly pronounced. 'Management consultants pretty well always mean sackings, of one sort or another. You know what that means, with plummeting circulation figures like ours.'

The management consultant turned up a couple of days later. He was posh, ruddy-faced, tow-headed, and his name, they said, was Giles. He got to work immediately behind his partition, on a tiny laptop withdrawn from a metal briefcase. He had powers, Sophie said, to snoop at the work on everybody's desktop computer. He was counting people's keystrokes, to see who was doing the least work. Lorna agreed with Sophie, it was all completely terrible, but to her secret self admitted that she thought it was good. It made work a bit more lively if you thought you were being snooped on. At least someone was taking an interest. At least there would be change.

Another memo appeared on the email. A sub-editor had been sacked for sending a page to the printer without a picture in its picture box, and a caption that still read WILL SOMEONE FIND A PIC OF SOME SAD FUCKERS TO GO IN HEREY HERE. Employees were referred to clauses in their contract of employment. Employees were also warned that there were to be no more taxis, unless the signature of a line manager had expressly been sought. Beatrice, Lorna noticed, had a new way of walking lately, whenever she had to pass you by. You could see her lift her head by clenching the muscles under her jaw.

Then the office was agog when two junior editors from the news desk were fired the week before they were due to finish their probation. 'They don't come cheap, these time-and-motion boffins,' said Julie. 'Looks like they're sacking the rest of us so they can pay his fucking fees.' A memo went round about out-of-pocket expenses: no out-of-pocket expenses to be incurred without express prior authorisation. 'That'll be express prior permission from a line dancer, sorry, line manager,' Julie said. Then there was a memo about unnecessary use of company mobile phones and pagers. Julie looked furious for a moment, then started fiercely typing a memo of her own.

The trouble with all this lopping was, it was making things lopsided. Jobs were mutating into each other, and going pear-shaped, and growing extra eyes. Boundaries collapsed. The organisation leaked energy. Everyone got tired and yet more tired.

Daisy got Kelly to help her organise a sale of all the free books and CDs sent in by publishers and record companies, most of which ended up under desks among spare shoes and old boxes of hanging files. The money would go to the leper colony, said Julie, laughing and shaking her swearie tin. The girls spent a couple of days rooting all the stuff out. Afterwards, they went off together for lunch.

'Off to scramble over a single lettuce leaf, are we, O skinny ones?' Julie said in her fond voice.

'He he he,' said Daisy.

'He, he, he,' said Kelly, copying her.

'Do you want to come, Miranda?' said Daisy, politely. Miranda said she simply couldn't, she needed to get on with her report. Actually Miranda was hanging about in the hope of catching the eye of the management consultant, who she thought was absolutely lovely. She loved his socks, she loved his white eyelashes, and she longed to hear more about the firm whose consultancy division employed him, which, unlike her current boyfriend's outfit, was said to be one of the big four.

'I bet Giles plays hardball,' she said wistfully, gazing over at the pinky-lilac plush partition.

What exactly is hardball? Lorna wondered to herself.

*   *   *

Over the weeks, a new gang was coming together around the brainy section, of shadowy, good-looking young people who thought they might try their hands at writing for a change. They were never the really famous people, though they might look like them, or claim intimate acquaintance, or have names a bit like their names. But they did live in that same raffish half-world of mad wealth and implausible careers: gallery owners who were also high-class drug dealers, party organisers who painted portraits of famous friends, restaurateurs who had authored bitter-sweet coming-of-age novels, the embarrassing younger sons of life peers.

The pieces, when they arrived, were uniformly terrible, though in a life-affirming variety of ways. There were factual errors, contradictions, untruths and half-truths. There were libels and unforgivable misspellings. There were mixed metaphors, danglers, verbless sentences. Lorna was astonished by the lack of care and scruple. These people weren't even trying. These people didn't give a toss.

'Christ, this piece here is completely hopeless,' Julie would complain in a loud voice to her audience in a general sort of way. She didn't speak directly to Lorna if she could help it. She still tended very much to avoid Lorna's eye. 'What a load of fucking bollocks. Why the fuck are we publishing this drivel, I ask you?' She did not seem drawn to answer her own question, or any of the other, progressively more exacting, questions that might have followed on.

It was like her forefathers, thought Lorna, in the Scottish Highlands in times of famine, in the freezing winters. The peasants did not kill their cattle for meat, they tapped the veins for warm blood to mix in with their oatmeal. They wore the animal down, they did not kill it. They got more protein and iron, in the long run, from their kine that way.

And something appalling was beginning to shine through the verbiage. There was a new page 2 slot called 'Gimme, Gimme, Gimme . . .'. There was one on the back page, called 'Why We Hate . . .'

*　　*　　*

123

Lorna rang Peter on his mobile, and was most surprised when, for once, he picked it up. 'My dear, come round and visit us for supper,' he suggested. 'Meet the children. Chew the fat. Let me hear about how you're getting on.' 'I'd be delighted,' said Lorna, then agonised for ages in the expensive wine shop in the mall. When at last she got back to the office, there was an email waiting. Something had come up, sadly, terribly sorry for the lack of notice. The lovely supper would have to be postponed.

Lorna riffled through the party invites Miranda kept on top of her computer in search of free champagne. She chose a book launch, quite a grand one, in an institutional building in the West End. Luckily she was wearing her trouser suit and her nice little boots that day. She ran into Robin Moody there, encrusted with a strange new glitter that was maybe success and celebrity, maybe just cocaine. He had a new suit, even more luscious than his old one, and a shirt a little too big for him round the collar. He seemed to be hovering round Daisy, who was dressed in op-art stripes and massive wedges. Or possibly, not mutually exclusively, Daisy was hovering round him.

'Aren't we looking grown-up these days,' Lorna said to him, rather sourly. 'Beatrice was looking for your mobile number,' she added. 'She didn't seem best pleased.'

'I sleep around with your workmates so you don't have to,' Robin said, giggling and looking at her oddly. 'My bonnie wee Lorna, what a glow you've got. You're looking really well.'

Peter never did come back to clear out his desk properly, so Julie inherited his files of correspondence, ignored and un-answered, going back for months and months. Sometimes, she read out bits of it, for entertainment, in the long and wearisome afternoons.

'"Dear Mr Pevensey. I have submitted five of these pieces to the agreed deadline, and so far, you have published exactly none. Nor have I received even the first instalment of the agreed re-muneration . . ."

'"Attention Peter Pevensey: for the third week running, you

have completely changed the argument of my column without consulting me."

'"Peter, dear Peter: so moved by our conversation. Shall we not meet again before too many weeks have passed?"

'"Ptr, simply cannot agree with yr remarks abt my article on S**** T******. It is ***essential*** I be seen t b admiring, his son goes to the same school as my twins. Pls call me abt this soonest, or I shall be forced to contact Beatrice. As ever, kind regards."

'I say, sirrah!' said Julie, laughing. 'Lorna, it's your pal!' She passed over a pile of written paper. Lorna knew it had to be to do with Robin before she came across his sheaf. There was a proposal for an article on nepotism and the Oxbridge nexus. There was a proposal for a page 5 essay, 'Whither the Working Class?' There was a proposal for a column, 'The Outsider'. Robin would sneak along as a gatecrasher into the smartest parties, asking impertinent questions of the great and the good. 'I have been in correspondence with one of your subordinates about these topics,' the covering letter said, 'but to no avail. Perhaps I can offer you a drink one evening, or supper, at my club?'

'I always said he'd go far, that boy,' said Julie. 'Up his own arse if not someone else's. Fnur fnur fnur.'

There was a changing scent around the department, of something growing to a fruition. Lorna looked around her, sniffing. It had to do with Julie, she was sure. She had a new and shorter skirt, which she wore with ribbed tights in jewel colours, dark red, dark purple, dark green. She had a new long black jacket with leg-of-mutton sleeves. Her hair got shorter, the pompadour flatter and flatter. Her eyes were no longer puffy. Her breath no longer smelt of drink.

Kelly, in the meantime, was getting thinner and thinner inside her bobbly black jumper. 'Kells, why do you always wear the same jumper? Not that we want to see your flesh particularly,' said Julie, almost kindly. 'You must get your shoes heeled, Kellster,' she continued. 'You're going to fall over on them one day, and break your skinny little bod in two.'

One day, Kelly did indeed fall over on those heels of hers,

causing her to slop Lorna's tea all over her pile of proofs. 'Oh Kelly,' Lorna said, quite nastily. 'Oh Kelly. For heaven's sake.' After she had said it, she sensed there was something wrong with the acoustic. She looked up to see her expostulation sink and fester, deep in the flesh of Kelly's back.

'I'm really sorry, Lorna,' Kelly snorted, in floods of weeping.

'Oh look, Kelly, for heaven's sake, come on,' said Lorna. An agitation she would never have noticed as a smoker built up around her ribcage. She had to discharge it deliberately with a deep and sudden breath. There was anger there, and a sadness. 'Oh look, Kelly, come on, for heaven's sake.'

Kelly's personality was fading on a daily basis, fading and diminishing under the weight of thick black spikes. Neuroses stuck out all over her. She was being pinched and torn apart with wires. Being a self-absorbed young person, the motives of other people were obscure to her. She started thinking there must be something terribly wrong with her that only others could see.

It didn't help that she had given up on Rilke and moved on to his anguished descendant, the Jewish Romanian poet Paul Celan, who lost both his parents to the Holocaust and himself spent his early twenties imprisoned in a Nazi labour camp. 'Black milk of daybreak we drink you at night / we drink you at noon in the morning we drink you at sundown / we drink you and we drink you,' Celan writes in his best-known poem, 'Death Fugue'. Kelly related to the poet personally. Paul, as she secretly called him, was a handsome young man, after the war, in Paris. He was a professor at the École Normale Supérieure. Black milk of daybreak, we drink you and we drink you: it would have been so much better for Kelly if she had been eating barley brose with Lorna, and learning how to proof-read properly, learning how to make her way. But she wasn't; she was sitting in her bedsit, dreaming of her Paul. If only Kelly had been around to help him, he would never have made that jump into the Seine.

She wrote a second version of her 'Philosophy is a Lover Too'

126

article, but this time, it didn't work at all. It was so dreadfully self-involved and self-enfolding, and it just went on and on. It was full of abstract words, and German words, and jargon. Sentences never made simple declarations, but were long and complex, hinged on colons and semicolons; their second halves contradicting and undermining the first. She was falling headlong into the awful pit at the very heart of philosophy. None of it means anything, at bottom, if you look at it too closely, and without the proper spirit. None of it means anything at all.

'These philosophers,' Lorna realised, as if she'd never noticed previously, 'they're just mad paranoid delusionists. It's just the maddest paranoid fantasy. All they do is, they just completely make it up.'

'The quintessence of the quiddity,' said Julie. 'The *flüssigkeit* of the *Fluss*. I can't publish this stuff, Kelly. It doesn't make any sense.'

Kelly looked from Lorna to Julie, from Julie to Lorna, and over to Daisy, whom she was hoping might be her new friend. She felt like one of those toys made of bits of cardboard, whirring as somebody pulls outwards on two opposing cords.

Lorna was invited along for a drink one day, with a new, young company that was launching a trendy website. She went in to meet the founder in a former warehouse building in Clerkenwell. The partition walls were painted lime green and orange. Lorna sat uncomfortably on a see-through plastic chair. 'The trouble here,' she said, sipping her glass of warm white wine, 'is there's an inherent contradiction in the technology. You don't need to update the eternal verities two or three times daily, and I think, really, it's the eternal verities I'm best at, probably. Eternal verities and spelling.' The money being offered was terrible. Lorna thought she was quite happy when they didn't offer her a job.

The following week, she pretended she had a doctor's appointment so she could go for an interview in north London, in a smart street of skinny terraces, just round the corner from where Peter Pevensey lived. It was a classy outfit, this one; Peter himself sat on its board. He had recommended Lorna for this job in fact, though not highly, Lorna got the feeling. The selection panel was listless. They already knew exactly who they wanted for this position, and it wasn't her.

Lorna was pretty certain that this was the first time ever in either of her lives that she had pretended to have a doctor's appointment while sneaking off to do something else. It was a peculiar feeling, heady, but also limited. Funny, she thought, if she were Julie or someone, she would do this all the time.

After, she walked past Peter's house on her way back to the tube station. It had a shiny black door with a fanlight, and steps, and railings, with little potted trees. The door opened and a small child came trotting out. Lorna hid her face behind her briefcase and hurried herself away. On her way home, she ducked out of the tube at Oxford Circus, and took a quick tour of the fashion displays in the great department stores. She found feathers and puffs and bits of embroidery; tottering shoes; hideous plenty. We're so going to come to regret all this, thought Lorna, though she could not have said why.

Back in her flat, she changed into her running clothes and trainers. 'Hello,' the young man in the dry-cleaner's said, appraising her with gumption, as Lorna's entrance made the bell on the door go ping. 'You have brought me your beautiful trousers?' The walls were covered with old-style rules and warnings on flashes of fluorescent cardboard. The young man was remarkably handsome, Lorna noticed. On her way out, she glowed and glowed.

The dry-cleaner's shop was at one end of a short parade on the estate's central shopping precinct. There was also a bookies, a post office and an off-licence, and a food store that sold only otherwise unheard-of cheapo brands. All the shops had grilles on their doors and windows. None of them was ever completely empty, but neither were they ever in any way full.

Lorna passed a bin and fished out an old newspaper, unfolded, fairly fresh. 'Estate of the Nation' was about Hegel, Lordship and Bondage: 'Work was the only power they had, the men of my granda's generation, and it killed them even as it gave them life.' 'And what, exactly, is the nature of your bondage, Mr Moody?' Lorna said to herself. A week ago, Beatrice had been over, asking bad-temperedly if he had changed his email address. She was brusque and did not look happy. She had the dearest little frock on, and Lorna had felt a bit disgusted. She dropped the paper in an oily puddle and ran on.

With the growth of nuance in her body, Lorna's mind, too, got more receptive to the shapes and surfaces around her. She ran around the scissor block on Phase II of her scheme, on the other side of the street; it had an actual skirt running round the bottom of it, like a hovercraft, where it joined up with the pavement. The skirt was most off-putting. It might have been a fence. The paths and walkways inside the estate did not properly join up with those outside it, you always felt you were crossing a boundary, pushing through a force field, going on to someone else's turf. And so, if you didn't have a manifest reason to cross it, you simply wouldn't, and that was that.

There was a place on her run where every day she smelt spicy fruity Jamaican pudding. Presumably it was being baked in an oven, presumably there was a baker there. She had never seen it and she would never think of going there. She would go to her own minimart, as she thought of it, or she would go to the high street on her weekly shop. She would never venture on to Phase II in search of fruity Jamaican pudding. Just as no one in the little streets of terraces would ever come and do their errands in the shops on her estate.

It would be good to take over one of those empty shops on the precinct and open something surprising there, an art gallery, a dress shop, a tea shop with fancy cakes. That was what Lorna could do with all her savings. She would open a destination restaurant on her shopping precinct. And then she would get married to the lovely owner of the destination dry-cleaner's next door.

She made another date with Peter, for a drink in a pub in north London, up by where he lived. He looked exhausted for some reason, really exhausted, but this time, he did not wriggle out. His face had a lardy look to it, of a sudden. His hair gave off a smell of stale cake. 'Why not write your masterpiece?' he suggested. 'Make some notes. Gather pebbles in a jar. A girl like you needs a plan, you know. You need to know where you want to go. You are surrounded by people who know what they want, and know it fiercely. If you aren't stronger than they are, they will suck you up.'

'Someone else said something like that to me,' said Lorna. 'That was Robin Moody. He said it to me, and all the time, he was actually doing it, to me.'

'Robin Moody?' said Peter. 'You mean *the* Robin Moody, the columnist and writer? Do you know him, then? He seems to be quite the young man of the moment. I didn't know Robin Moody was a friend of yours.'

Lorna smiled non-committally. Peter suddenly coughed.

'That reminds me,' he continued. 'You wouldn't have a copy of Hegel's *Phenomenology*, would you? For some reason, it's sold out all over London. For some reason, it's suddenly quite the thing.'

That night, she had a dream in which she saw Daisy bent over her computer, working on a spreadsheet made up of symbols in the place of figures or words. Down the sides there were arrows in different thicknesses and directions. Everyone was there, everyone, divided into sheep and goats. Along the top were the pictograms: an eye with big lashes; a light bulb; some sort of abstract flower; an outline star. The body of the grid was filled with ticks and crosses. As she watched, Daisy keyed in a single red X where the eye met with a fat black bendy arrow. The whole thing flipped over to display row upon row of blank, corrupted data: OOCOCOCCCOOOOXXXXXXXKKKKKKKOC OCOCOCC COOOO XXXXXXXKKKKKK: O COCOCOCCOOOO XXXXXXXKKKKKK.

'The trouble is,' a voice like Daisy's said – a voice like Daisy's, but grave – 'it's all a bit unstable. I'll keep at it, though, and we'll see what we can do.'

'The ledger of our souls,' thought Lorna, clearly, and with an awful inevitability. 'The ledger of our souls.'

'Daisy,' Lorna asked the following morning. 'Do you ever do data-processing work for Lady Beatrice?'

'Just started cleaning her house at the weekends, when she's away in Scotland, if that's what you mean,' said Daisy. 'Fabulous house, really fabulous. Something to aim for, know what I'm saying? Something to give you a reason to believe.'

'You work as a cleaner for Beatrice as well as working here?'

'Well, I wouldn't be able to live in London on what I get paid for this job, would I? The pay's much better than when I cleaned these offices here, so I don't need to do so many hours? Don't need to steal so much toilet paper neither?'

In a way Lorna had been right then. Daisy was in on something. Daisy in some way was in on whatever was really going on. That night, Lorna stole her first ever roll of toilet paper from the office toilet. She just took her bag into the marble cubicle and stuffed the roll right in. As she waited for the lift, she felt like a criminal. Then, when she walked out on the open concourse, she felt like a young god.

The next day, a sign went up on the toilet door:

DUE TO PILFERING BY PERSON'S UNKNOWN,
TOILET PAPER WILL BE DOWNGRADED TILL
FURTHER NOTICE.

Lorna booted up her computer to find a sinister memo on the email:

Lorna: the editor-in-chief would like to meet you, next
Monday morning at 11 a.m. Please see me if this time
is not convenient; otherwise, confirm.

Looking up and fearfully around her, she caught the eye of Beatrice, who seemed to be watching her, and Beatrice smiled her bonny smile. She looked over at the empty corner and, sure enough, there was the management consultant, watching Beatrice with a frown. She ran her fingers over her face and felt a newish pimple, throbbing with anxiety. Here it was then, the change, at last. Here it was at last, the change.

That night, she stayed on in the office for a long time, thinking, reflecting, making notes. The light was yellowish and smeary. Every hour a security guard came round and nodded. Outside it was completely dark. Her plan was to collate all the thoughts she had already had about the paper, her analysis of its contents, her new and better ideas, and get them down on a single side of A4. Then she would take that with her, into this sinister Monday meeting, and the editor-in-chief could like it or lump it. The editor-in-chief could like it or lump it, and Lorna would take things on from there.

Right now, though, she was bored and getting nowhere; and so, she wanted to smoke. Instead, she went for a walk round the edge of the office, breathing deeply and looking at the ranks of lighted windows in the flats beneath her, and beyond them, the bendy yellow strips of motorway disappearing into the greatest of all the tunnels that runs beneath the Thames. She slipped through a gap in the pinky-lilac plush-covered partition and walked round the empty zone, where the Observatory shone like a single oil lamp in the middle of Greenwich Park. A lone figure was hard at work on the sports desk, the TV set mounted above him emitting a dull hum. Little trapdoors opened in the grey carpet with sockets for cables and lines.

A cardboard box in a corner had the remains of the World of Conflict map on the top of it, and an old *Who's Who*. Lorna bent over to see if it was worth saving, and flipped the pages to look at her own surname, nestling cosily like a cuckoo among the great and the good. None of these knights or judges bore any relation to her whatsoever, as far as she could remember. Just looking at the name, though, made her feel a little warmed.

Julie, she noticed, had left her desk in chaos, with Robin's disgraceful sheet of proposals lying on the top. Lorna wondered if she had left it like that deliberately, with a secret security camera trained on it, hidden somewhere behind the roofing tiles. Julie had also left behind her a neat pile of business cards freshly printed with her name and position. Lorna felt a stab of fresh new envy when she saw them. She had to hold her arms down tightly to stop herself knocking them over as she passed.

The next day was Friday, and when she woke up in the morning, she could not bear to go in. She gargled to make her voice croak then phoned up and said she was sorry, but she thought she had the flu. 'You remember Miranda had to go to the doctor,' said Daisy, laughing, 'and Jules isn't in yet, she says the tube's gone down. Funny if me and Kelly have to do the lot of it. He he he.'

Daisy went on with her work in the meanwhile, sorting out the post. There was a letter from the leprosy charity, thanking Julie for her generous donation. The amount of money mentioned was very much less than what had been raised by the recent sale, but happily for Julie, Daisy was as careless with numbers and maths and stuff as she was with everything else.

Chapter Ten

What a pity, though, that Lorna chose that Friday of all Fridays to go awol. Miranda was out all day at the doctor, and Beatrice had to leave the office early to get to the country for the weekend. 'Fuck this for a game of soldiers,' said Julie, clearing off a couple of minutes after, leaving Daisy and Kelly to close the edition on their own. Daisy had to get to her West End bar job by 9 p.m. on the dot, which meant she had to leave at eight. Kelly sat on, like Cinderella, releasing final versions of the pages, until just before midnight, and somehow, something went askew on the server and the wrong version of the page 3 people piece went off.

It was meant to be an interview with a lovely young artist who had just written a tearful memoir about her former lover, acclaimed by all as the great man of his generation. She was a sweet girl; the photograph was beautiful, the lovely artist, in dungarees with no top underneath them, standing in front of a portrait she had painted of the old goat himself. Instead, the printer got Julie's customised photo of Peter, savaged, with carbuncles and a bolt through his neck, and a big splash head-line, thus:

Come Sunday, Kelly didn't even notice what had happened. She had never actually bought a copy of the paper in her life. Julie didn't always buy it either. But she did have Beatrice on the company mobile at nine o'clock that Sunday morning, shrieking. 'Look on the bright side, Bea, one day it'll be a collector's item,' Julie quipped from her bedside, where she had been lying in her negligee, the horsehair pad she used for her pompadour sitting atop the nearby chiffonier. No one ever called Beatrice Bea like that, to her face, as it were, from so low down on the social pecking order. Beatrice shrieked and shrieked again.

'Why is it,' Julie started come Monday morning, 'that everything you touch has this funny way of going wrong, Kells? Why is it? Why is it? Can you answer me that?'

Kelly looked at her, horrified, her face sunken and her eyes gone huge.

'Why is it, you have all these degrees in philosophy, and yet you don't seem able to do anything right at all? Why aren't you bumbling about in some library or something? Because you're a bloody reject, that's why. Because they didn't even want you there.'

'I'm sorry,' said Kelly. 'I'm sorry.' She remembered *The Little Book of Depression*. 'I think I might be a bit depressed.'

'Jesus Christ almighty, she's a bit depressed now, is she! Handy little excuse! Well, I feel a bit depressed just looking at you!'

'Well' – Kelly foolishly ventured – 'I feel a bit depressed just looking at you as well, you know.'

'Kelly answering back, is she! Kelly answering back! Speak up a bit, will you, Kells, none of us can hear you! You are just such a pathetic nightmare, you're just a complete and utter disaster. You're completely fucking useless, you know that. You really are a complete and utter waste of space.'

135

Something broke off the side of Kelly and scuttled away into a corner. Miranda and Daisy just sat there, shame-faced. They needn't really have worried though. Things were going dreadfully by now, all over the paper, and no one much beyond their own tight-knit and inward-looking gaggle had time or energy to pay any attention to their troubles at all.

'Jules went completely ballistic,' Daisy explained to Lorna later. 'So Kells just got up and ran out of the office, I think she was crying, and that was the end of her.'

'Did it not occur to you to run after her?' said Lorna. 'I thought Kelly was supposed to be your friend.'

'Well, she is my friend, sort of,' said Daisy, 'but you know, she really is her own worst enemy. Just like Jules says she is? She is. She really is.'

'Well, she's not her own worst enemy with you around, or indeed Julie, is she,' said Lorna. 'It isn't Kelly's job to sign off pages, it's Julie's, and if Julie hadn't done that horrible picture in the first place, it would hardly have ended up on the page. You know perfectly well that she's lazy and she's a bully, and why she is tolerated in this place is a mystery. You should all be bloody ashamed of yourselves. It just isn't bloody fair.'

She sat herself down at her desk and booted up her email. Train brakes and violin strings were screeching in her head. She created a new memo, for the attention of the editor-in-chief and Beatrice; then she thought for a moment, then she copied Julie in on it as well. 'FRIDAY FUCK-UP', she called it, and then she considered how to start. Advice from somewhere floated into her head: count to ten before you react to anything, and call your stressor by the name of a favourite flower. Lorna couldn't at all think of the right sort of flower, so she changed the filename to 'LITTLE BUNNIES' and thought on.

'Lorna.' It was the adorable PA, come over to her desk. 'Lorna. You're in with the editor bloke, the editor-in-chief bloke says he'll see you now.'

Lorna had forgotten about her meeting with the editor. It was supposed to be in half an hour. She glanced again at the smart folder she had prepared for it, her ideas marked out in tables, with bullet points, and it gave her the right idea. 'Actually, I'm not going to see the editor this morning. Actually, I'm out of the office today. If you want to talk to me about all this, you had better phone me later. Right now, I'm going to see how Kelly is, and then I'm going home.'

She sat herself down deliberately in Miranda's chair and pulled the top-of-the-range rotary file-card-holder towards her. She flipped through the little cards with their pretty rounded writing, found Kelly's address and phone number and copied them down. As she put the card back, she noticed the entries it slipped on top of: K for Kennedy (JF, John, 'Jack'), Kigali, Kosovo. J, as well as being for Julie, was for Job, as in Book of, and Johnson (Samuel, 'Sam'). L for Lorna was also for Lampedusa and Lloyd George.

'Evil, evil, the evil of human evil,' Kelly said to herself as she lay there, over and over again. 'Evil, evil, the evil of human evil.' She found that just saying it brought her some relief. Kelly was lying in bed in her nasty bedsit, in the desert hinterland between King's Cross and Camden Town. She still had all her clothes on, her socks and her trousers and her bobbly black jumper. The bed was clammy and the sheetless mattress was stained. The duvet, in its unlovable brown sprigged cover, was over her to her neck. Kelly tunnelled further backwards in her pillow. She was an organism under attack by wicked phages. She was a twitching purple blob.

'Who, among the ranks of angels, will hear me as I cry?' thought Kelly. 'Who, among the ranks of angels, will hear me as I cry?'

She had taken to bed with her favourite book of the moment, a popular mystical work about how the global consciousness of humanity was gradually evolving into a new dimension, in which the world would at last become the better place towards which it has struggled since the dawn of time. 'The New Culture Revolution', the chapter she was reading was entitled. 'The transformation of the actual from the possible; the moment the world becomes infused with spirit, healed by the power of human love.'

The Rilke sat, with Celan and a couple of others, on top of a broken-down chest of drawers. It was white, with gilded loops for handles and worrying brown smears. The lock didn't work on the front of the bow-fronted old wardrobe. Creak creak creak, went the wardrobe. On the other side of the window, starlings in the trees by a row of broken-down warehouses sang.

Kelly opened her eyes and looked around her, and wanted very much not to be awake. Cough medicine, she had discovered, was helpful. It made her sleep, and it gave her wonderful dreams of cold, white alpine ski slopes, with dark tracks and fir trees and sinister little cardboard cut-out figures sneaking off round the back. And so did cough medicine mixed with bargain-label vodka, sometimes sweetened with bargain-label cola and sometimes not.

'Evil, evil, the evil of human evil,' Lorna thought, looking up from the street at the front of Kelly's building. Her heart wobbled a little, then braced. Here she was, she had decided to do this, so she had better just do it with all her might.

Kelly's digs were in a yellow-brick terraced house, its front wall obscured by scaffolding and with a view out over railway lines across the road. The interior had long ago been converted to make as many rentable rooms as possible, causing calamitous structural damage, which was now beginning to show. Kelly's room was at the back of the house, off the second-floor landing, next door to the communal bathroom. Floorboards creaked under a baggy sponge-backed carpet. The door was locked and Kelly didn't answer, but it was only a piece of chipboard with a rubbishy lock in it, easy enough to slip.

'Oh, for heaven's sake, Kelly,' said Lorna, sighing. 'I'm going to sit down on this armchair, and I want you to get up.'

She looked around her, sizing up the situation. It was all so tremendously familiar, the details were difficult to grasp. There was Kelly lying in her bed with her clothes on, covered by the brown quilt with its utterly hateful flowers and branches. Who had ever designed such a pattern? What had the brief been, the fee paid, the constraints? The ugliness of the room, thought Lorna, was not helpful for a young woman with depression. But then, these things go round and round in rings. A pile of ash was entirely Kelly's doing, heaped like droppings along the fold of an old scorched newspaper. So was an empty cheese packet filled with cigarette ends on the floor. The brown cord spongy armchair was a little bit damp and smelly. Lorna had the oddest feeling that she had sat before on this very armchair, not in this room but another one, many, many miles away.

'If I lived in a place like this,' she said loudly, 'I would lie there pissed in my bed as well. But, Kelly, you silly cow, how are you going to get out?'

'I'm so ashamed,' Kelly whimpered. 'This is the worst thing ever. I'm so ashamed of myself.'

'Yes, well, so, I suppose you have to imagine,' said Lorna, 'that this is as bad as it gets, pretty much, Kells. So you've had your moment of humiliation. Now it's time to start on the up.'

Kelly threw her head back on the pillow and made to pull the flowered quilt over her head. 'She really hates you, Lorna, she really hates you. I don't know why she suddenly started hating you like that, but now she really does.'

'Who are you talking about, Kelly? What are you talking about?'

'She keeps going on about a crime ring, and how you think you're pure as the driven snow.'

'Julie,' said Lorna, 'For heaven's sake, Julie. If I were you, Kelly, I wouldn't pay much attention to that Julie and her rants.'

'Oh, and Miranda hates you too, you know. They say terrible things about you when you're not there. Miranda is compiling a dossier on your underground activities, to hand in to Lady Bea.'

'My underground activities, for heaven's sake! And what exactly would they be?'

Kelly shook her head. 'I've seen it, though, she keeps it in a special folder.'

'Miranda keeps many things in her special folders,' Lorna said, with a snort. She picked up a plastic carrier bag, half tucked under the brown cord armchair. An open tin fell out of it, of sicky-pink bodybuilders' protein shake. 'This is no good, Kelly, eating all this junk,' said Lorna. 'We are going out for a constitutional. We are going to the launderette. We are going to buy you some vegetables. But first of all, I'm going to stand outside while you take a bath in that horrible bathroom, and fill a couple of rubbish bags with all this crap you've got in your room.'

Lorna turned her back while Kelly stripped her filthy clothes off and put on another outfit, a scruffy old black T-shirt and a pair of ridiculously baggy snow-wash jeans. 'Wear your trainers,' Lorna suggested, kicking them out from under a pile of dirty underwear. 'I think, on our way to do your washing, we should have a ceremonial disposal of those bad-luck boots.'

Sitting there and waiting in the brown cord spongy armchair, Lorna noticed that she had folded her hands in her lap. She had, she realised, that special formal calm feeling, that momentary freedom from the problems of the self. It is the gift the rescued gives to the rescuer, this feeling, if only either party knew it. Except that egotism on both sides causes it to be misrecognised as the other way about.

They dumped the washing in a machine round the corner then went next door to a Turkish shop with a beautiful display of yellow peppers. Clouds were piled in the sky like paradise, white and bubbly with yellow edges. 'Beans and pulses, Kells,' said Lorna, picking up a sack of chickpeas. 'Good for protein, good for roughage, good for self-discipline and the soul.' This theory came to Lorna, in a flash, as she was speaking. Most beans and pulses have to be soaked overnight before you cook them, which means that eating them involves a bit of forward planning. And forward planning means self-discipline and faith in the future, that it will come, most likely, if nothing else.

'Well, it's a poisonous business,' Lorna had been saying. 'We're a failing organisation, in a historically redundant sector, so what would you expect? Look at us, what a shower we all are.'

Kelly started to laugh compliantly, then stopped. 'I am a shower, Lorna,' she said. 'I can't do anything, really, can I? I mean, look at me, I'm a disaster, Lorna. I can't do anything useful. I really can't.'

'Well, I'm not sure that any of us do anything useful, exactly,' said Lorna. A board outside a café offered coffee, tea, waters and juices; a tiny table wobbled on the pavement. 'Why don't I buy you something to drink? We're knowledge workers, it's supposed to be a knowledge-based economy. This city's supposed to be full of work for people like us to do.'

'Lorna,' said Kelly shyly, 'do you think I've got what it takes to make it as a writer? Do you really think I've got what it takes?'

'I'm not sure that's a question much worth asking,' said Lorna. 'If you want to be a writer, shouldn't you just write stuff and find out?'

This is more or less what Rilke says in his *Letters to a Young Poet*, lying neglected and getting curly on Kelly's chest of drawers: 'There is no one who can advise or who can aid you: no one. There is only one way: you must go inside yourself.' But then, Rilke had not been troubled by the problem of interest piling up on student loans and overdrafts. Rilke had not had to worry about grooming, rising house prices, the problem of getting a boyfriend and so on.

Kelly had written a paper for that professor at the university: 'Rilke's Letters: Solipsism, Exchange and the Law of Random Reward'. At that time, she had been interested in the way the work of art appears to transcend the normal fetters of the commodity relationship: that there, even more than in other areas of advanced capitalist relations, the financial rewards for effort come out totally arbitrary and out of proportion to the volume and quality of labour put in. It's as unpredictable and unfair as the love of the old gods for their favourites, she had written in one of her attacks of inspiration. It's as undeserved as mercy, as mysterious as grace.

'Maybe you need to start off small, like Miranda does,' said Lorna. 'You know, those index cards.' They were walking past a newsagent's, so Lorna popped in to see if she could pick some up. She found the cards, next to the brown envelopes and the Chinese notebooks. 'Robin Moody, Inside', was advertised along the top of the snooty paper. 'The Award-Winning Columnist on the Sickness Unto Death.'

'I mean, look at you, Kelly,' Lorna was saying, as she wiped with a scrap of newspaper round the two-ring hob. 'Peter said you were a prodigy. So why not just be one, for heaven's sake?' She was amazed to find she could talk so much, waving her arms around, without smoking. 'I mean, you're perfectly capable, I know, I saw the first version of your essay. Why don't you try this writing lark then, if that's what you think you should do with it? Why don't you give it a wee bit more of a go?'

The hot, clean washing gave Kelly's room a lovely high detergent smell. The sun shone in through the dirty window, through the backs of draped damp sheets. Lorna was making her lentil soup with chopped peppers; she thought she'd do a salad with cheese for afters. She scraped carrots with a bendy plastic dessert knife. She washed a Turkish lettuce and arranged it on a tray that someone, at some point, had stolen from a pub.

'I mean, Lorna, why did they teach us all that stuff if there was no point to it? Why do they pay the teachers' wages? Why do they pay for the upkeep of the libraries? I mean, what is it all for?'

'Well, I suppose they don't so much any more, really, do they?'

142

said Lorna, sitting back down on her brown cord spongy chair. The backs of her legs were sticky from dampness; the wet lurking deep inside it had risen in the warmth. 'I suppose these arts and humanities courses when you think about it, the training's high-volume and pretty cheap. I mean, there's always plenty of really keen people desperate to go into law and business. I mean, if everybody wanted to be a lawyer, the system would collapse. So I suppose if you want to do philosophy or whatever, that's great, that's fine by them, they'll just pay some other useless individual a pittance to mark your essays, and so it all goes round and round.'

'That isn't what you think, really,' said Kelly, looking suddenly a little tearful. 'You think philosophy's really important, the be-all and end-all as you call it, the most important thing in the world.'

'I'd rather you didn't tell me what I do and do not believe,' said Lorna briskly, turning down the heat to the lowest simmer.

'Yes but look, Lorna, look.' Kelly lay across her bed on her stomach, her arm stretched out to scrabble in the gap between the top of the mattress and the wall. 'Look, Lorna, there it is,' she said, pulling out the tatty sheet of paper that had fallen down the back. 'To make the world philosophical, that was Hegel's world-historical goal . . .' It was quite a big sheet, A3, bright-white copier paper; it looked like a page proof to the brainy section, except that in the space waiting for a nice big photo, someone had inserted that terrible picture of Peter Pevensey, with the monster bolt and the carbuncles, and some-thing extra, superimposed on top. It was an image of a hand, outstretched, open, reaching forward to grasp. It was the opposite gesture, as Lorna realised, to the socialist clenched fist.

'Let me look at that,' said Lorna dully, her own hand reaching out. BOSSES BEWARE, it said on the upper deck of the main headline; WE'RE WATCHING YOU, it said on the second deck underneath.

'I found this stuff on the photocopier,' said Kelly proudly. 'I spotted it and I thought, shit, someone could get into a lot of trouble, so I thought I'd better take it home.'

'I wrote this stuff, didn't I?' said Lorna, shaking as she looked. '"Human nature is alienated, but contains within it the possibility of and desire to get beyond alienation to transcendence, the be-all and end-all of all human action and culture.' Oh dear, oh dear, oh dear,' said Lorna, feeling an alarming dawning feeling, of horror and excitement mixed. 'I wrote this, didn't I? This is pretty well all my own work.'

'To make the world more philosophical, by reading more philosophy, you know, I thought, that's what I think, that's what I do, really, that's what I've been doing all my life,' said Kelly. 'I hacked into Julie's computer to see what else there was, she's mad, you know, keeping stuff like that on her desktop. I guess I must have been making automatic backups, and that's how that thing ended up going to the printer's. I don't really think it's fair, though, for Julie to put all the blame on me.'

'"We must alienate ourselves from the sources of alienation, build layers inside layers inside layers, and so, the tissue of the tunnel of our escape,"' read Lorna, in a rising fug of shame and pride. 'What was the plan, then, what was the bloody end point? A spaceship, a secret escape hatch, a time machine or what?'

'I wanted to put bits in, you know, when I was writing my article, but I thought I'd better talk to you or Julie first. But the two of you were always so intimidating, I never had the nerve to ask you. I was always too intimidated. I tried to loads of times.'

'"The absolute otherness of the other,"' read Lorna, in an ecstasy of mortification. 'Yes but, Kelly, it really is the most awful rubbish. I mean, I wrote it, unfortunately, I should know. I mean, it's pretentious rubbish, written by a pair of students who've been drinking far too much bloody coffee. I mean, just a pair of students, with their useless eighties educations, pissing their grants away on too much political theory instead of living life.' Lorna remembered her coffee mug of the 1980s, it had a Nicaraguan peasant on it, she saved up the vouchers from the backs of packets. She always wanted to go out there, as some others did, to help the Sandinistas with their coffee harvest, but instead of that, travelling and working outside in the open air, she had always ended up indoors, hunched and smoking, struggling and labouring, trying to get it right.

'"A movement, to live inside the skin of the yuppie, but secretly, planning the escape, not only our escape, but that of the entire society around us,"' Kelly recited. 'Isn't that what you're doing now, Lorna? Isn't that sort of what working at the paper's all about?'

'God, I hope not,' said Lorna. 'No, Kelly, I really don't think so, I think I would sort of know.'

'So doesn't the movement exist at all, then?'

'I don't know,' said Lorna, sadly. 'Maybe they have coffee mornings or something, and for some reason haven't invited me.'

'But you must be up to something, surely, Lorna? You can't just be sitting there rewriting those moronic articles, I mean, can you, for heaven's sake. I mean, you can't just be doing it as if that was your life's ambition. I mean, you can't be doing just that and nothing else.'

'Oh can't I?' said Lorna, feeling snappy. 'And what am I supposed to do for money, pray, given the usual constraints?'

'I mean, I know you were up to that thing with Julie, I heard you talking about it, remember, that time just before you had your row. You were up to that secret thing with Julie. I heard the two of you discussing it just before you had that enormous falling-out.'

'I don't know, Kelly,' said Lorna, vanquished, like an enormous bucket of disappointment had just been dumped on her head. 'I don't know anything about Julie or anyone else. I've lost my memory, I think I've had a brainstorm or something. I don't know anything, really, about the past.' She shook water off the pepper and sliced it up tiny, pulling off the whitish innards as she went. She piled up the red bits for later on top of the soup pot then turned and snapped the cooker off at the wall. 'Look, Kelly, there's your index cards, on the table. I've got to go now, I've got an appointment. Look after yourself, will you, and I'll call you tomorrow morning first thing.'

Kelly waited until Lorna had thumped the door behind her. Then she got up and fetched the bottle of bargain-label vodka she had hidden down the back of her broken-down chest of drawers. She ate all the cheese so she wouldn't have to think about it later. She filled a mug with vodka sweetened with sugar from a sachet and skipped happily back to her sheetless bed.

Kelly also had a book about the Nazi death camps, which she liked to read over and over, looking for something in it that didn't seem to be there. She pretended her interest was intellectual and scientific, though really it had to do with an awful need she felt inside herself, and did not for the life of her understand. She sensed this also, though she would never have admitted it. She maintained it had to do with modernity, and political systems, and the abysmal hole at the centre of the European mind.

'"Black milk of daybreak, we drink you and we drink you . . . Black milk of daybreak, we drink you and we drink you . . ."'

Kelly sank back in her slimy wadding pillows. For a moment, they felt perfectly gracious and cool and dry. She tried to get her thoughts back to where they had been before she was interrupted. She sank into a delicious dream of pits and mud-people, and herself, Miss Kelly, the only pure force for truth and social justice, the saviour of the world.

These days, Lorna always carried her trainers about with her, so she changed into them on the train. Her mind was swollen up and rancid. Things were coming back, coming back. She remembered perfectly the dialectical page proof, and now that she remembered it, what seemed strange was all that time that she had not. She remembered damp kitchens, a mouldy smell, a dirty old fitted carpet; she remembered more nights of slaving at a toadlike computer, the same toadlike computer as the one that sat on her table now.

And of course she remembered being bosom friends with Julie, a warm, excited feeling, with alcohol in it, and plotting, and street markets and bric-a-brac, and sitting at high stools in trendy bars. 'Have one of mine, m'dear, no, no, go on, have one of mine,' said Julie. 'Have one of mine, m'dear, no, no, go on, have one of mine,' said Lorna merrily, and then the two of them cracked up.

At the top of the escalator she gave her travelcard to the young man who hung about there, taking people's tickets then attempting to sell them on. Groaning, almost, in her bones, she started to run along the main road. You go around with this idea, she thought, that people don't really do terrible things to other people, it doesn't really happen, you just think it does because you're warped. You even see it sometimes, you bear witness to it, except that you don't believe what you are seeing. You see it, but you don't see it. You don't believe the evidence of your eyes.

She was jogging on the spot at the traffic lights when across the road she saw a couple of youths picking on another one, a smaller boy, who fell to the ground. The youths stood around him, kicking, looking bored. Lorna leapt from the kerb to save him. She didn't notice the white van rattling round the corner, too fast over an unfamiliar junction. The driver noticed her, though, and finally swerved to avoid her. Lorna fell over on her side.

'I'm fine, really,' she kept saying to the lady who stopped to help her. 'Are you the driver?' she said to the paramedic, who was strapping her on a stretcher. 'Are you going to put me in your van?' 'I'm fine, really,' she said to the triage nurse at the hospital. 'Ped vs van RTA, pain +++, ?#LEFT (?right) tib/fib,' the triage nurse wrote on her form.

147

Lorna lay for hours on a trolley, watching tunics and clip-boards, always rushing on their way to someone else. 'Are you all right in there?' a nurse would pause to ask her sometimes. Lorna would nod then shake her head. She could see her bones in the air in front of her, grey and greasy with flared ends. She could feel a shocking agony where lines of nerve ends no longer quite joined up. A man came in, a cocky doctor, and moved her leg into different positions. Lorna could tell what was going to happen before he made it happen, and when it did, she screamed.

Loaded up with painkillers, Lorna dreamed that all of them in the office were actually one and the same person, with differ-ences only in the props. Kelly was dressed up as Miranda, except a different sort of Miranda, with a sequinned bag and an auburn beehive. Daisy was Julie, shouting in a Julieish fashion, except with lots of Daisyish glottal stops. Julie was pantomiming Peter, wearing a pair of plastic spectacles joined to a false nose and moustache. 'It's a dialectic, innit,' a divine voice declaimed over the credit sequence. 'Each of us is on our way, now and always, to becoming someone else.'

Lorna was still euphoric the next morning. She asked the nurse for a payphone to be brought to her bed. It rang and rang, and then Daisy answered. 'I'm in the hospital,' said Lorna. 'I'm going to be on crutches. I'm in pain.'

'Oh dear, oh blimey, poor you,' said Daisy, laughing, as though the day before had never happened. 'Hey, you'd better get well soon, though, so you can come to my leaving do.' Daisy, like Lorna, had been in for a drink with the people at the website. Except that Daisy, unlike Lorna, had been offered a wonderful new job.

A clever physio with an agency badge on brought Lorna a pair of lightweight crutches and watched her, applauding, as she swung like a burdened monkey. Swing doors banged with trolleys laden with folders. Doctors shouted out the names of patients who were not there. Lorna longed to flee for that other world of black cabs and smooth terrazzo flooring. Except that

148

she couldn't flee it, could she, not with her leg encased in a cast.

'That's you, young miss,' said the cocky little doctor. 'Is your pal coming in to collect you?'

'I haven't got a pal,' said Lorna.

'Better get a taxi,' said the cocky doctor. 'And work on the pal bit, they have their uses from time to time.'

The cab dropped her off at the main door of her building. The driver watched as she got her good leg out, and then her crutches, with her broken leg coming last. It was a hot day, the height of summer, nearly. On her way back into the darkness of her building, Lorna's crutch slipped on a bit of chicken. The lobby, for some reason, smelt of stinking fish.

What with the broken leg and all the upset, Lorna completely forgot to phone Kelly, as she had promised. When eventually she remembered, Kelly answered right away.

'How on earth do you expect me to get better if you keep letting me down like this?' said Kelly, in a whiny voice. 'Why should I even try to get better if you can't even keep your word?'

Lorna explained, briefly, about her afflictions. She could feel Kelly receding as she was talking, a smaller figure and a smaller, at the end of an infinite corridor of flapping doors.

Kelly came off the phone and lay down again in her swaddle. She hadn't bothered even to put the fresh cover of her duvet back on. She tried to get back to where she was in her book about the Nazis, but for the moment, the spell was gone. She pulled down her curling Rilke and started reading again where she had stopped off, so many months ago: 'Alas, who is there / We can make use of?' Rilke asked.

Not angels, not men; even animals can tell how unsure of ourselves we are; but

There remains, perhaps,
some tree on a slope, to be looked at day after day,

there remains for us yesterday's walk and the long-drawn loyalty
of a habit that liked us and stayed . . .

Yesterday's walk, thought Kelly; yesterday. She started going
through her clothes drawers, searching for her scary elasticated
skirt.

Chapter Eleven

To think Lorna had thought that when she jogged, she inter-
acted with the world around her. She must have been barking
mad. Now she had her leg in a cast and crutches, now she really
understood it. Now she really lived in her building. Now she
really was involved.

The steel door was so very stiff and heavy, now she wasn't
letting it bang behind her to stride off along the winding
pathway. The lift could be so, so slow in coming, now she had
no choice but to wait for it, and wait for it, and wait. She got
terribly scared sometimes, standing there, alone and crippled
in the dark, empty undercroft, hearing shouting lads
approaching. She dropped a crutch in her nervousness; it skidded
along the floor.

But she had timed it well really, her leg had caught the short
hot part of the summer. The sunlight glared through the
unscreened windows. Insects threw their bodies in gangs against
the glass. A lot of the time, she lay on her bed, her eyes shut,
keeping her leg up, just thinking. Sirens rose from the street so
far below her. Towels flapped along the washing line, fright-
ening the pigeons from settling on the roof.

It had all been such a laugh at first, with Julie in her council flat, back in the days when Lorna was still new in London and Julie was her friend. 'Life not work,' said Julie, and Lorna typed it. 'Work is hell,' she said, so Lorna typed that as well. 'Bosses beware,' said Julie. 'We will shake you to your foundations. Your offices are our hotbeds of radical discontent.' Whose offices? Lorna wondered, still typing. The ones we work in daily? The ones we depend on, kind of, for our daily bread?

'We are everywhere around you,' Julie continued, 'in your corridors, your lifts, your glass-roofed atria.'

'Isn't that a wee bit threatening?' said Lorna, peering at the paper.

'So are we or are we not a revolutionary movement?' said Julie, wagging her cigarette in the air in front of her. 'Threatening is good.'

Lorna thought back somewhat further, to her long-lost student days in Scotland: Edinburgh, with its low, bulky horizontals, its sudden vistas of hills and rocky cliffs. There was a stall on Saturday mornings in front of the supermarket by the student union, with leaflets, posters, badges, demonstrations. She remembered friends and other comrades, Sheena, Ewan, Audrey, Nahid. She remembered her elfin flatmates, dancing along the floorboards with their heavy boots and their funny haircuts. She remembered the long, long nights of labour, at a clattering carriage to begin with, then later, at a dark and green-lit screen.

Then lurking at the bottom, Lorna saw something very clearly: a basement flat, painted in thick colours, somewhere on the eastern side of Edinburgh's handsome Georgian New Town. She was leaning on a photocopier, the old sort with a floppy cover, smoking a skinny roll-up. She could actually see herself, had she really been so very tiny, wearing black leggings and a baggy T-shirt. Her hair was bleached and tufty. She was looking out of a window, tall and narrow, at the street above her. It was dull and raining, as back in those days, it so often was.

A girl was coming down the steps towards her, oilskin shooting jacket and wellingtons, tipped-up shirt collar, pearls. A scruffy pamphlet with the unclenched fist on its cover poked out from her poacher's pocket. She held a spiral-bound notepad in her hand. It was Lady Beatrice, long before her brilliant marriage, in the days she was trying out as a reporter on a London society magazine.

'So, Lorna,' Beatrice said, in the deep, low voice she affected even then. 'I wonder if you can spell it out for our readers. What does it really feel like, being an anarcho-communist refusenik? What does it really feel like, being part of the embittered generation, Thatcher's Rebels, the generation that has given up on hope?'

'Oh get stuffed, you silly goose,' said Lorna, sucking ferociously at her skinny roll-up. 'Oh you silly goose you, will you just get stuffed.'

Now that Lorna found herself disabled, the smallness of the studio came into its own. She planned a soup with what remained of her vegetables, a special soup with potatoes and an extra swirl of pepper. She could do with new vegetables, really, but she couldn't see how she would get them. A pain of loss and bottomless sadness hit as she was filling the pan with water. She pulled out the rotten bits from her bunch of parsley and went on.

The mornings were so dark up there, that was always the trouble; the mornings were so cold and dark that winter, with electric lights on and the curtains drawn. You felt hung-over although you weren't. There always seemed to be cigarette smoke in the room. Lorna got a grippe or something, and was so ill, she couldn't clear it. Cold and darkness encroached from room corners, dropping like webs from the cracking high old ceilings. The only colour came from Lorna's dried-out old green high-lighter pen.

Lorna lay in her bed in climbing socks and a sleeping bag, with her smelly old duvet tucked round. Her flatmates, the pretty anarcho-communist pixies, wandered in and out of her room, but could not be depended upon for food. Lorna would put on an Aran jumper, a dead-granny coat from a thrift shop, the sort of clothes people wore at the end of the 1980s, before synthetic fleece and breathable nylon came in. She boiled water in a pan to fill her hot-water bottle. She left the house only to buy bargain-label orange juice and cans of soup.

For months and months, it felt like, Lorna wandered around in a dwam as the Scottish people call it, speaking only sometimes when spoken to, smiling only sometimes when smiled at. She fed herself on glossy drama, women with blonde hair and luminous faces, stepping in and out of glittering skyscrapers, striding along the plunging, overshadowed Midtown streets. She nestled in the moments before the cameras started rolling, the dark spaces between scenes and moments and after the theme song welled up at the end. She longed for a suit with built-up shoulders and shiny buttons. She longed for that blowsy fullness of rabbit-tail bleached hair.

Lorna had been noticing for some time already that the movement of souls in the Edinburgh flat around her was coming to have a pattern. People came, people left, people hung around. Over time, however, the main movement was one of leaving. Over time, Lorna's comrades and flatmates were gone. It must have been shortly after that, she thought, that she caught a train for London, and had her first deli sandwich with Julie, cackling and mocking, the two of them, in one of the city's old Italian cafés. Afterwards, they went round a tatty street market behind the law chambers and the diamond merchants. Everywhere you went you heard Neneh Cherry and Soul II Soul.

And it must have been shortly after that, figured Lorna, that Julie had helped her get established, letting her sleep on her living room futon, getting her a part-time job at the radical bookshop just round the corner from the paper where she worked. Lunchtimes, Julie wandered in to visit her, and to shoplift the odd serial-killer story, the occasional feminist thriller, whatever caught her eye. Lorna, meanwhile, was busily stuffing her stormproofed Scottish rucksack with beautiful shiny editions of all the great modern works: *The Protestant Ethic and the Spirit of Capitalism*; *The Philosophy of Money*; *The Jargon of Authenticity*; *One-Way Street*; stolen with a compulsion almost industrial in its effects. She stole the books but she barely read them, just hoarded them in boxes in a corner. She stole them for the poetry of their titles, and a distant promise that poetry seemed to contain.

'He's just such a complete and utter fucking bozo,' Julie was saying, the anger turning her face and distorting it in the blue-tinged mirror tiles on the pillar. 'Pevensey the Putrid. Peter Poodle Poetaster, the Pathetic Fallacy Made Flesh.'

Lorna was sitting on her bed in her underwear, admiring her leg in its cast. She had been such a twit, the day she got that first phone call from Peter Pevensey, in the mid-to-late 1990s, when she was subbing for an agency, her days of working in the radical bookshop faded from her mind. 'Lorna, my dear, I got your name from your old chum Julie, she sings your praises to the skies. We need a girl to come in and start here Monday, and Julie said you would be the very thing. General knowledge, perfect spelling, the ability to work like a little Trojan. It's very difficult these days, finding someone with an eye both for the humble comma and the wider sweep.'

'Here we are, Lorn, at last, your bid for stardom,' said Julie, a couple of days later, over celebration coloured ciggies and cocktails in the bar. 'Not for the first time, I save you from the slushpile; I'm your great big fairy godmother, that's exactly what I am. It's brilliant here, it's total chaos, Lorna. We can use the photocopiers and printers for anything we like.'

To begin with, Lorna had high hopes of her wonderful new job. It was a joy to travel to the wharf of a morning from her bare, plain old starveling life in south-east London. It was so good to take up a position on the mid-to-late 1990s panorama, a shiny head with boots and shirts and a job to go to, a person with a career. 'Bosses beware,' she typed in happily, on a collage she was making for Julie's birthday card. Bosses beware, for the workers are watching you: they are waiting for you to blunder, then they will steal your job.

'It's just so unfair,' Julie was saying, that alarming night in the turquoise cocktail bar. 'I mean, he's just completely fucking crap at the job, you know he is. I mean, you and me could do it on a jobshare. I mean, it's just so unfair.'

'I mean, I agree with you, he's a bit of a wally,' said Lorna, puffing away, admiring her hollowed-out cheeks on the pillar. 'I mean, yes, of course, he's completely hopeless. Yes, of course it's not really right.'

'I was thinking,' said Julie, 'of arousing your interest in a *coup d'état*. A sort of palace uprising, if you will, remembering your revolutionary interests of old.'

Lorna wondered why Julie was talking like a person in a film.

'Against Peter, you know, against the Pevensey monster. Imagine it, Lorn, if we could only get him fired.'

Lorna sat on, practising avoidance tactics. 'Isn't that a wee bit over the top or something?' she said, for want of anything else.

'We could do it on a jobshare, we could be the fucking dream team. We could be our own little crime ring, like when you worked in that shop.'

Lorna sat there, saying nothing, nibbling at the side of her glass. The pillar reflected a face with a smile on it, a small smile, in a slot.

'I don't understand you, Lorn,' said Julie with a lurch. 'You're supposed to be the radical round these parts, but here you are, you know, sucking up to the hopeless public-school wanker. Here you are, Comrade Lorna, sucking up to the public-school wanker. You're such a fucking bully, you know that, Lorna. You're such a fucking moral bully and prig.'

Lorna sat on, doing her smiling. 'Don't you think, though, Julie, you're being a bit over the top?'

She looked up and saw Peter on the far side of the pillar, laughing and gesticulating, out for a drink with his cronies from the sports desk. He caught her eye and pretended that he hadn't. Julie was right, of course. It really wasn't fair. He was tall and handsome, plausible and popular. He was not tormented by the inner presbytery of stern elders, telling him that whatever he did it was never good enough, and never, ever would be, quite. He didn't worry about secret reckonings and final judgements. He was Peter Pevensey and everything was marvellous. Everything was lovely. Everything would be fine.

Julie followed her eyes and saw him also. 'Oh, I hate him, I just wish he would get cancer,' she said, with a horrible vehemence. 'Put the rest of us out of our misery. I wish he would just get fucking cancer and die.'

Lorna's leg ached in its plaster as she remembered. Already she was on the phone to Peter, calling. How ever could she have forgotten. How ever could she have forgot.

The Friday night before the brainstorm, Peter slipped off at around half past five. 'Well, gang,' he said, with a hangdog look around him, and a secret shrug for Lorna, which Lorna didn't see. 'I have to go to my appointment. Everything's in pretty good shape here, Lorna, if you wouldn't mind holding the fort.'

'Fuck this for a laugh and giggle,' said Julie, picking up her bag and making to leave straight after. 'Anyone coming? I am repairing to the pub.'

'You can't go now,' said Lorna, horrified. 'You haven't finished your work.'

'You didn't say that to Pete, for Pete's sake. You never said that to Pete, for Pete's sake. Fnur fnur fnur.'

'But that's different, innit,' said Lorna. 'He said he had an appointment. These things happen, it's what we're paid for, after all. He said he might have to leave early, he said it in the Monday meeting. Only you wouldn't know about it, because you weren't there yourself.'

'Righty-oh, then, Comrade Lorna, now would seem the time if ever any time did for the oft-discussed *coup d'état*. But I suppose you're too much of a wimp to contemplate it, even. Are you too much of a wimp to contemplate it, even? Thought so. Tatty bye.' And so, with Daisy and Miranda staring hard at the floor as they walked behind her, Julie had fucked off.

Lorna walked over to the basket by Beatrice's office and looked up Julie's proofs. She had sloped off, as Lorna knew she would have, leaving her pages unsigned, and with stupid mistakes all over. Lorna sat down and worked her way through the worst of it. It didn't take her long. It took her a great deal longer to compose the email she then sent Julie, full of pent-up fury from years and years. 'You are your own worst enemy,' was how this email started. Getting it right in every detail took until just after half past ten.

Lorna left the office at eleven, so she never knew that Julie came back from the pub shortly after, read her message once with a sorry sag of the shoulders and emailed it straight back to her. It was waiting for her, at the top of her inbox, when she got in on the Monday morning, swollen and exhausted from a miserable weekend. She read it once and then she lost it, never, ever again to find it. She read it, her finger slipped, and she lost it, never once for a moment thinking to search for it under Sent.

Robin Moody had a new picture of himself at the top of his column, no longer 'Estate of the Nation', now simply 'Robin Moody Writes'. The new picture didn't have the public-housing backdrop. It was just Robin in profile, looking noble and faintly steely, brewed in Scotland from girders, as the advert said.

Robin had developed a new and annoying affectation of using the expression 'my people' in his column when he meant his family, or his readers, or the Scots in general, and using it a lot. Lorna's leg itched like hell inside its plaster every time she even thought of it, with irritation and envy. On the one hand, she thought it dreadful stuff, really dreadful, and that one day, Robin would so come to regret it. On the other, at least he was writing, at least he was doing things, at least he had cracked the problem of how to earn a decent living. At least he wasn't stuck in a top-floor flat in a hateful plaster, hobbling downstairs to buy a pint of milk and a paper. At least he was out there, making progress, moving on.

'He was a dour man, my granda,' began the column. 'He would have hated me even so much as mentioning him in the boss-class newspaper . . . I need to tell his story now for his sake, and for the sake of his people.'

'You need to tell his story now,' thought Lorna, 'for the sake of your fee.' She was thinking about a safety pin she had seen trapped in the crack between two floorboards. She was imagining it dropped inside her plaster. It would be lovely and cool to begin with. Later, she could use it to tear up all the bits of itchy skin.

'For my granda's story is also the story of this whole country,' Robin Moody continued, 'and the men who worked to build it, only to be abandoned and forgotten when their youth and strength was used up.'

'Oh, for fuck's sake,' snorted Lorna, as she threw the newspaper on the floor. She hated the way Robin's face swam up at her through the ragged rows of newsprint. She hated the way he was forever feeling the pain of other people, taking it over from them, making it his own. He could be writing about his granda; he could be writing about some girlfriend; he could be writing about the global fate of the industrial working class. It didn't matter who the victim was for that week. Robin's writing was all about himself.

What Lorna was too angry to appreciate was that this was Robin's special knack. His column was like a magic mirror, reflecting back to his readers an image of himself, sort of, rippled over an image of the reader as the reader would like to be. What a great kid, what a lovely idealistic youngster. What authenticity, what compassion, what heart. Readers felt guilty and regretful about all the things that Robin's writing sort of stood for: the poor, the elderly, the sick and industrially injured, the obsolete and frankly fucked-over working class. They felt guilty and regretful, with a horrible nagging feeling of dread somewhere in there too. Robin's column allowed people to enjoy their regretful feelings, to feel them less as a burdensome worry and more as evidence that they themselves must be caring people, they were feeling so many feelings, after all.

Except that it didn't work on Lorna, blocked and furious in front of the toadlike computer. In Lorna, the image of Robin sank straight to the very bottom of the dank Calvinist puddle of her heart.

As time went by, her leg muscles wasted away a bit, which meant there was more room to get a properly abrasive instrument down the sides of her cast. She spent half a day untwisting a wire coat hanger from the lovely dry-cleaner, then poked it down and scratched. She was trying to get it all down at her computer, trying to write it out in steps. There was no sound but the breathing noise her computer made, and the clicks of her fingers on the keyboard. The single bulb got weaker and weaker. The dark around the table thickened and grew strong.

It took Lorna no time at all to write up her ideas about the brainy section, which she typed up on the toadlike computer and mailed off to the editor-in-chief. It took her much, much longer to come to terms with her memories, all the trouble of the past.

She found a set of eighties postcards with awful social-realist images of happy peasants marching to work with their hoes and their machetes, then later on, in battledress, waving their pennants from the tops of tanks. She found payslips and bank statements, letters from the Inland Revenue and the National Insurance Contributions Agency, electric bills and gas bills and phone bills and tenancy agreements: so much evidence of frantic saving, so much evidence of monies paid out in rent. She found notes and drafts and bits of writing that made her flush from her top end to her bottom. There were notes towards a Marxist account of the Hollywood movies of the eighties, with mad fantasy interludes meant to illustrate the return of the repressed. There was an aphoristic iconography of Margaret Thatcher, with dream sequences and a parallel analysis of sadomasochism in philosophical accounts of the ideal state. There was a list of possible titles, all with the word 'dialectic' in them: 'Hollywood Dialectic', 'A Dialectical History of London', 'Dialectic of Thatcherism', 'Anger: the Dialectical View'. But it is a dialectic, isn't it? a freshly agitated Lorna started wondering anew.

The weekend just before the brainstorm, she had sat, as usual, in front of the toadlike computer, looking back at the screeds and screeds of notes. All through Saturday and on to Sunday morning, she flicked through files and folders until suddenly she saw at long last what the story was really all about. It was a sad tale of self-delusion, self-importance, self-indulgence. It was a tragedy of one young philosophy student, sidetracked and seduced. By Sunday evening, she was working away on a new fresh version, fuelled by cigarettes and instant coffee, and chocolate biscuits from the minimart up the road. By early Monday, she was making the last great synthesis when suddenly the electricity went phut.

She had been tired, she remembered, so tired, with an infinite dryness. Her head was clanging, clanging, with noise. There had been pressure, and a flickering, and a failure. She had a bath, she ironed her good shirt, she made her way to work.

Stir-fries, Lorna considered, were the best food for a woman in her position. Loose leaves, dried rice and noodles, small things like garlic and ginger, food that relied on condiments she already had in the house. The things to avoid were bulky roots, such as potatoes and onions, and tins and pulses, and fruits, unfortunately, most of their weight being water. But she did stagger most days to the Turkish shop for a single grape-fruit. Thinking about when she would go out to do that gave her days a focus apart from her brooding and fretting about the past.

She could manage her rucksack, sort of, carried on both her shoulders, so long as it only carried a lightish load. Lettuces she could hold in carrier bags, clamped in place by her armpits. She looked like some sort of a folding gadget, with her two aluminium crutches and her untidy load. People looked on disapprovingly, like there was a law against food-shopping if you are at all disabled. Everyone thinks his or her own troubles are the worst and most urgent in the world.

Lorna's heart dropped to see the epaulette couple approaching. The man looked even iller than he had used to. The woman was perhaps a little fatter, but she was smiling, which was new.

'Fell off our motorbike, did we, girlfriend?' said the woman.

'I don't have a motorbike,' said Lorna crossly. 'Now, were you going to offer me some help or what?'

'We weren't,' said the woman, 'but I suppose we could do, if you need a hand.' She stood on for a moment, then moved forward. 'Where's the boyfriend then, when you actually need him?'

'I dumped him,' said Lorna, 'quite a while ago. Did he not drop in to see you, like he said?'

'He came the once, didn't he, Joseph? Remember him, that twitchy geezer, sniffing around for drugs?' The lift came and the woman arranged Lorna's bags in the cleaner corner. 'You'll be better off without him, mate. Come on, girlfriend, going up.'

'So what did you do, jump out the bloody window?' said the man in a quiet voice, with the quietest of smiles. 'I did that once, Christ, it was bloody agony. Not my finest hour.'

Lorna looked at him straight, for the first time ever.

'But that's nothing, mate, compared to having your flesh torn apart by small horned devils,' the man said, smiling wider.

'No, I suppose it wouldn't be,' said Lorna, at a loss. She looked at the woman properly for the first time also, and the woman looked at her. 'I'm Lorna, by the way,' said Lorna. 'I can't really offer you my hand.'

'Angela,' said the woman Robin had called Melanie; so at least he had done her neighbours the courtesy of not using their real names.

Lorna noticed the archive in the library when she went in to skim the past week's papers. A woman brought a box file to her table and helped her fix her leg up on a chair. A council employee had started the archive in 1957, as the very first tenants were settling in the very first completed blocks. It had press cuttings, costings, a report by London County Council Architects, manually typed on long, thin sheets of foolscap, so difficult even to handle these days, after three decades of A4. The six twenty-one-storey point blocks would be the tallest buildings south of the river. The budget for all of them together came to £1,138,343. The rent on a studio such as Lorna's was £4 weekly, heating included. A picture in a local paper showed the alderman handing the keys to the very first family to move in: a man and a lady, and a little girl with pompoms on her woollen hood.

She washed her face and combed her hair down before she took her trousers, ripped and stained from when she had fallen over on the road, along the footpath to the lovely dry-cleaner. It took her ages to get there on her crutches. She stopped underneath the triumphal archway and put on powder from her compact, with a touch of mascara for her eyes.

The bell behind the door rang, but there was no one behind the counter. A door at the back of the shop stood open, and behind it, the living room. The television was on a satellite channel, a news show with a disaster on it, and a clock in the corner, and words in a foreign tongue. There were bunk beds with children sitting on them, and a sofa bed pulled down. A woman in a bathrobe turned and saw her. Her face was green and streaky and worn out.

163

Lorna turned to leave but the lovely man had heard the bell and came rushing, closing the door to his family life behind him. Lorna could see that he was desperate, although he tried to do his usual smile. She gave him her beautiful stained trousers, he gave her a yellow ticket. She longed to fill that room with fruit and flowers, all the bounty of the world.

Chapter Twelve

Things were much more fun, though, out on the wharf, with its landmark tower, where business was beginning to boom again as the mid-to-late 1990s went rolling on towards their end. Rents were up, on both office space and retail. Work had begun on Phases II and III across the water. A new arcade of high-street fashion stores had opened in the basement, with a couple of top-end estate agents and a conveyor-belt sushi bar. A staircase had been excavated from the atrium for access, with wide steps swooping downwards and an ugly beaten-bronze balustrade.

By now, however, the complex was beginning to sink into the rising water, under the weight of poor materials, slipshod calculations, squares confused with square roots. There was too much building above to be supported by the piles underneath it. There was movement as they settled and the movement pushed drains out of kilter, leading to unexpected cracks and blocks. New gaps opened between the smooth white world of the basement's insides and the darkness all around it; disaster might have followed, but that the contractors became aware of the problem just in time. Engineers laboured all night in the deadliest of secret. Men worked from chains and cradles every weekend.

You would think they would never get away with it, finding hazardous errors in the structure of the very building in which a newspaper was housed. A worried site worker, a conscience-stricken project manager, would tip off the news desk, surely: you would think so, but they didn't. An eager reporter, bristling with eyes and ears, would notice something odd and overactive in the pattern of cranes and blocked-off walkways on his daily route from the train; you would think so, maybe, but no. Columns were braced, cables retensioned, shiny panels stuck on top of joins, and no one on the paper even noticed. Champagne went on puddling round the cracks and gutters. Rains fell, the river rose, hot and cold fronts sloshed across the sky.

It was so strange, going back into the office, swinging along on crutches after a couple of weeks away. The carpet was terribly grey, she noticed. The desks and cabinets were just so horribly grey and smooth. The ceiling was even lower than she remembered, she could knock out lighting units with her crutches. The piles of paper were dead dry, going curly, ready to be burnt. But Miranda had been in early to do her office flowers. Her vase marked the brainy section like a beacon, seasonally filled with a spiky pinky blossom offset by angry twists of bamboo. Only, the vase had moved, to the desk that Peter used to sit at, opposite Lorna's; and so had Miranda, Lorna saw. There she sat, glum and anxious-looking, nibbling at the ends of her hair and copying entries from an online database into her personal rotary filing system. It looked as though Julie and Miranda had fallen out over something, and Miranda had taken it hard.

'Hi, gang, I'm on crutches,' Lorna said, fake-dazzling, as she limped past Julie's desk. 'Long John Silver, not,' muttered Julie, shaking the swearie tin and squawking. 'Who's a pretty girl, then. Pieces of eight.' Julie's hair was in a bob now, almost; the pompadour had gone completely, to be replaced by a bouncy fringe. She didn't look well on it, however. Her face had new shadows on the downstroke of the cheek.

Lorna's desk was heaped high with unopened mail and faxes,

with an overspill cascading to her chair. 'Is Daisy in?' Lorna asked Miranda, looking round.

'Oh, Daisy's gone,' said Miranda. 'They'd never given her a proper contract, had they, so when she heard she had that job with that e-commerce start-up, she just walked. I have been managing her duties in addition to my own, Lorna, but I can't be expected to do that indefinitely. I need to have a chat with Julie about this issue, Lorna, but she's not engaging with the task at hand at the moment, she doesn't really have her mind on the job.'

'Surely Kelly can help you?' said Lorna, dread growing as she said the words.

'Oh, we haven't seen Kelly here for ages. She could be dead or dying, for all that she's bothered to tell us.'

Lorna picked up a memo from Beatrice:

> As of now no expenses will be reimbursed FOR ANYTHING unless the claimant has prior permission, EXPLICITLY IN WRITING, from me. Please submit TO ME an itemised breakdown of likely costs BEFORE you incur them; otherwise, reimbursement cannot be guaranteed.

Clipped to it, Lorna saw, was her last expenses chit, with ???? all over every item. 'SEE ME,' Julie had scrawled on the bottom in red marker, as though she were the headmistress and Lorna was the dunce.

Lorna marched, as best she could on her crutches, straight over to Beatrice's cubicle. 'What's this all about, then?' she said to Daniel, the adorable PA.

'Oh, hey, Lorna, welcome back and all that,' the PA said, scratching his bottom through his French-cut pants. 'You'll have to fill in a sickness form, let me get you one. You did go off without permission, innit, so we'll need to get that ratified for you.'

'I didn't go off without permission,' said Lorna. 'I went and broke my bloody leg.'

'Here's the sickness form, Lorna, just fill it in and I'll get it processed for you. Get it in quickly and hopefully you won't get too much of your money docked.'

Lorna limped back to her workstation and swept the heap of mail to the floor. She leaned across and turned on her computer then sat back to watch the machine configure. Someone had left a pen without its cap on top of her keyboard. A nasty red stain was spreading across the front of her most excellent white shirt.

'Right, that does it,' said Lorna, picking up her crutches. 'I've had enough of this already. I'm going round the shops.'

Lorna heaved herself into the trendiest of the stores on offer, its window lurid with purple uplighting and skinny mannequins in magenta frocks. Bored thin girls stood round a fibreboard counter, packing poorly finished clothes in layers of tissue. Lorna picked her way through racks and racks of accessories, feathers, beads and rhinestones, nasty little bags and belts. 'I'd like to look at this one, a size smaller please,' she said, picking up a shoe she could already tell was hateful. 'Do you want both of them?' said the assistant, with a disdainful look at Lorna's leg in its dirty cast. She could hardly walk on her own feet, her shoes were so ill-balanced and extremely pointy. Her shoulders sagged forward as she edged her way to the storeroom, where the laminated flats and fittings gave way to dustballs and pads of invoices and loose wires.

Back in the office, all the desks were empty, as though after a bomb scare, and only Lorna had not been informed. Everyone was bunched up around the glass wall by the corner, staring outwards. 'What's happened?' she cried, swinging over. 'It's Lady Bea,' a man said, opening a space for her at the front. 'They've fired her, at last they've bloody fired her. The editor-in-chief just fired her after reading that guy's report.'

Lorna pushed through so she was standing flush to the window, looking down across a chasm to the roof of the building across the road. Sure enough, there was a helicopter, and sure enough, there was Beatrice, her hairdo covered by a silken scarf. She looked up and seemed to see her former hirelings, half a dozen storeys above her, some of them waving, some of them stamping on the floor. A look of intense dislike distorted her lovely features. She seemed to curse and shake her fist.

'Lorna, the editor-in-chief would like to see you,' said Beatrice's PA a little later, half snivelling, half giggling, torn between utter thrilldom at being in on something a bit exciting and abject terror at what would happen to him next.

'Thank you, Daniel,' said Lorna, a little distant, thinking. 'Thank you, Daniel. Just let me hobble over to my desk and I'll get my notes.'

The editor-in-chief sat in a corner office much the same as the one that had been Beatrice's, but over on the other side of the office, with views towards the tall buildings of the city's ancient financial centre, three or four miles up the river to the west. He smiled keenly when Lorna arrived on her crutches and rushed to fetch her an ottoman on which to rest her cast. The management consultant was sitting in his office with him, a copy of Lorna's memo open in front of him on the desk.

'My dear,' began the editor-in-chief in his careful accent, 'did you ever meet young Giles here, who's been my eyes and ears?'

The management consultant stood up and smiled and stuck his hand out. 'Not personally, although I believe he may have been snooping on my emails,' said Lorna, sitting up a little straighter and giving him a stare.

'We loved your report, both Giles and me,' the editor-in-chief continued, still smiling. 'Very lively, very sparky, and I think you're right, dear, something had to be done.'

Giles smiled also. 'Something had to be done, didn't it, Lorna? That had become extremely clear. This organisation has been functioning without a memory, is the way my firm would describe it. This organisation has not been functioning in an intelligent way.'

'You'll be glad to hear, I'm sure, we've been talking to Peter Pevensey; he speaks of you in the highest possible terms. You'll be glad to hear, I'm sure, we've persuaded him to come back.

We know how fond you are of him and how well the two of you work together. We're asking you to fill in for the next month or so, until Peter can get started. It's a rarity, a girl like you to have such an eye both for the humble comma and the broad sweep.'

Lorna was glad she had practised being silent so much. Without her having to think about it too much, her face went blank.

'A cross between Leo Tolstoy and an au pair, is what that chap needs, and that's just what a girl like you can be. A cross between an au pair and Leo Tolstoy. We thought you could implement bits of your report together. We thought you'd find that fun.'

'You want Peter to take his old job back,' said Lorna, 'and you want me to assist him. You want us to implement my report together. You think I'll find that fun. So what's your plan for Julie, then? Where's Julie going to go?'

'I can't tell you yet because none of this is public. But here's a word in your ear. I've just had Julie in, I've offered her a senior management role. Get her off the hands-on stuff she's been getting bogged down in. Get her looking at strategy and finance. Promote her out of harm's way.'

'So you're promoting Julie because she's hopeless,' said Lorna. 'You're giving Peter his job back. You want me to stay where I am. You think my report was lively and sparky. You think I'm a cross between Leo Tolstoy and an au pair.' Lorna tried to think herself out of her body to see if this was one of those hothead things she would regret, like the long-ago incident with Lady Beatrice. 'But I don't regret that. Not really,' came the not-entirely-helpful reply.

'You'll get a pay rise as well, of course. We really thought you deserved that, after all you've tried to do.'

'Oh, get stuffed,' she thought of saying.

'Oh, get stuffed,' she actually said.

When Lorna got back to the brainy section, Miranda and Daniel were standing looking awkward. Julie was slumped at her desk in a bundle, shuddering and weeping, hugging the ridiculous Wowser to her chest. 'I can't do this, I don't want to do this,' she was saying. She was sniffing, and her nostrils were reddened. She saw Lorna, limping along on her crutches, and she burst out weeping again. 'Lorna, I'm just so, so sorry,' she was saying. 'Lorna, I'm just so, so sorry. I didn't mean for all this to happen, I didn't mean it. I didn't mean it, you have to believe me. I don't really know why it all went weird like this.'

'Well, it looks like it has, though,' said Lorna, icy. 'I can't imagine what you want me to say.'

Julie looked up at her imploringly. 'Lorna, you know better than anybody, I didn't mean for this to happen. Lorna, you know better than anybody, this isn't what I meant. I can't do this, I don't want to do this, Lorna.'

'I do. I will,' said Miranda. 'I've been meaning to have a chat with you, Julie, for a while. I've been collecting a dossier of your entertainment expenses, as passed on to me by Daisy, and I've been logging how often you come back from your lunches in no fit state. I was considering a chat with the management consultant, but he was always so busy with Lady Beatrice. I now intend chatting to the editor-in-chief direct.'

Miranda picked up her pretty folder and marched off with it round the corner. 'She could get you sacked, you know,' Lorna said to Julie, aware of a thin-lipped mercy rising through. 'I don't care if she does,' said Julie in a small voice. 'This job's been doing my fucking head in. I never meant for it to be like this. Look at me, Lorna,' she said, putting her hands out in front of her. 'I'm completely covered in warts and verrucas from the stress.'

In her eagerness to steal Julie's job from her, Miranda forgot to quit out of the database she had been working on at her screen. Lorna considered deleting some of the most important-looking entries on it but that, in spite of everything, seemed wrong. Instead, she sidled over and quickly added a couple of new ones, fictional names with fictional occupations and addresses. Emma Woodhouse she gave the position of CEO and managing director at Woodhouse Lydgate Associates, Corporate Branding. Gregor Samsa she put in as a freelance journalist, health & fitness & men's fashion, with a made-up address in Lower Clapton, London E5.

*   *   *

171

'You're very sick, aren't you,' she said to Peter a couple of weeks later. 'I'm so sorry, you know, I had a brainstorm, somehow, I just forgot I ever knew. I am so, so sorry. I don't know what else I can really say.'

'I thought I was supposed to be the absent-minded one,' said Peter, laughing and shrinking a little as the movement brought on the pain in his ribs. 'But never mind, my dear, let's forget it. Let's forget it!' He laughed again. 'I'll make us some tea, shall I?' he said, turning his face to hide a sudden cramping. 'My wife took the kids out shopping, they should be back any minute. I'd so much like it if you'd stay and meet them at last.'

They were sitting in Peter's kitchen, a beautiful stone-flagged basement hung with shining pots and pans. A shelved recess held whole rows of travel guides and cookbooks. It also had Lorna's *Phenomenology* in it, resplendently brainy-looking between a guide to Venetian churches and a pile of magazines. Lorna didn't like to mention it, not with Peter there, in his anguish. She left it for him to get round to the subject when he was ready, except that being Peter, of course, he never did.

'I should be good for a few months once I've had this round of chemo,' said Peter, cutting slices from a magnificent fat and yellow cake. 'And I know it sounds awful, Lorna, but you know, these school fees. I thought I'd work another month or two, and then, you know, I supposed I might get sick pay. I suppose you think that's reprehensible of me, Lorna. The trouble is, they were offering me so much money. They were really making me an offer that would be difficult to refuse.'

'Well, I'm not going to tell on you, if that's what you're worried about,' said Lorna. 'Go ahead, as far as I'm concerned, and good luck to you. Take them for all you can.'

'I can see it's all beastly unfair to someone like you, though,' Peter continued. 'They just like me for some reason, what can I say? They haven't a clue about what they're doing, so they'll pay through the nose for someone that makes them feel better about it as they're doing it. And look at me, so strong and handsome . . .' He broke off to laugh and shrink once more. 'Have

172

some cake, my dear, the nanny made it, the girl's a wonder and an angel. I can't eat that sort of thing at the moment. I cut both those pieces for you.'

'So what can I do to get taken more seriously? What would you advise me to do next?'

'I don't know,' said Peter, thinking. 'Isn't there some way you could marry in? Double your contacts and resources. What about your young friend Robin Moody?'

'I think I missed my chance with Robin Moody,' said Lorna. 'Or rather, he missed his chance with me.'

'I'd marry you myself, Lorna, except that I'm already taken,' said Peter sadly. 'No, I don't know what you can do. I suppose you could always get your teeth fixed while you're waiting for a better opportunity. I mean, your teeth are fine, my dear, they're really splendid, but they're a bit of a giveaway. You know.'

Lorna's leg was out of the cast now, an odd new combination of stiff and bendy. 'Well, anyway, I told them they could stuff it,' she said, flexing it in front of her, as much as she could. Peter smiled and reached for a horse-tablet. 'I don't know how the hell you think I'll manage without you,' he said.

The front door opened in the hall above them. 'Daddy, Daddy, see what I've got,' a little girl was yelling, rushing for the stairs. Peter stood up and made a strange face. Heels were heard to patter across a polished floor.

She called Robin Moody on his same old mobile number and was amazed when he answered right away.

'I think you owe me a lunch or something, don't you, Robin?'

'OK, then, Lorna,' he meekly said.

He turned up early, wearing heavy spectacles, and this time, he looked tired. He ordered a naked steak, he said he was on a special diet. He drank a single glass of wine.

'Aren't you going to have the whoreson pasta?' Lorna said pokingly, for old times' sake.

'You mean *puttanesca*?' said Robin blankly. 'I very seldom eat sauced pasta dishes now.' He smiled, and dug into his pocket.

173

'Look at this, though, it fell off the corner of that restaurant, you know, that party you had there,' he said, drawing out a chalky pebble. 'It's Portland stone, the real stuff, look, it's got a wee fossil in it.'

'Bonnie wee fossil,' said Lorna, trying to look solemn. 'I study you glout and gloss.'

'It just doesn't get any easier,' Robin told her, blinking. 'Old problems just get replaced with new ones, right enough.' He paused to let Lorna ask him about his troubles, but she decided just to sit there, saying nothing, wagging her foot against the leg of her chair. She felt a horrible hemmed-in feeling. 'What's your column about this week, then?' she eventually asked.

'Religion,' Robin said, looking doleful. 'Religion, and whether it's no, in a world without politics or ethics, probably all we've got.'

'I didn't know you were religious,' said Lorna.

'It grows on one, I find,' said Robin, his eyes beginning to get wet. 'It grows on one, as one continues the struggle with life's pain.' Lorna wound her calf round the back of her chair leg in order to keep it still.

'My bonnie wee Lorna,' Robin said, looking downcast, then swooping up to her eyes. 'What went wrong between us, eh? My girlfriend, you know my lovely girlfriend, she was saying how much she used to admire your moral courage . . .'

'I beg your pardon?' said Lorna, feeling sick.

'There's a bit about you in her book, I think, you know, that book she's writing, the one she got all the money for. You were a real pal to my Kelly when she needed one, Lorna, and I for one will never forget it. I'll never forget it, and isn't it amazing, the twists and turns life takes. Isn't it amazing, Lorna, that wee good turn you did for my girlfriend, immortalised in a book.'

Poor Kelly had had a tragic, dysfunctional childhood, apparently, and had plangent, poignant observations to make about what happens when the young and vulnerably brilliant mistake sexual depredation for the blandishments of love. Her memoir of the period, *Philosophy is a Lover Too*, was published a year or so later, to considerable fanfare.

'It's less a memoir as such, more an aphoristic configuration,' Kelly would say to Lorna at her launch party. 'The epigraph comes from Rilke, you know, he was always one of my favourite poets. I was also greatly influenced by Paul Celan.'

Oh, Lorna finally realised. So really, it's me who's the loser in this game then. Really, it was me that was the main loser all along.

Kelly's launch party was held out on the wharf, on the forecourt of the newly completed Underground station at Phase II. The mighty architect had moved away from his previous interest in infantile amorphousness to a revived espousal of ultra-rational forms. The space was cold and white, with horribly exact edges, like the area under the curve of an equation. Lorna glanced uneasily up the escalators to the chilly glazing high above them. Bombs, beams, bits of masonry would come down crashing through the roof and would roll straight into them down the shiny metal stairs.

Kelly's book was small and neat, like the author, and came in a turquoise dust jacket with a retro fifties design on it of ferns and shards. Copies were arranged on a console table with a stiff flower arrangement behind it, other-worldly horns and trumpets. Daisy was there, in astonishing shoes and a clever skirt suit. Peter by this time was dead. Robin had just abandoned Kelly for America, but she had barely noticed yet, she was so pumped up with drugs and excitement. Her book was acclaimed, she was a personage of fashion. '*Wir trinken und trinken*,' said Kelly, drinking. 'My main influences, as I may have told you, are Rilke and Paul Celan.'

Julie arrived, invited by Kelly, who for the moment loved everyone all the time. She wore her black lace mantilla and she had proper forties shoes on, high-topped lace-ups, with heels. She had moved to the south coast after she lost her job on the paper, investing her pay-off in her very own gift shop. Its name was Poshlust, done out in seashells, in punk-rock ransom-note lettering. As Julie said, and she said it often, it was the perfect name for a shop.

'Oh, we made life hell for her, really, now I look back on it,' she was saying to the publisher's publicity person at the party. 'Oh, we made sure she suffered, all right. It's a hard life, but somebody has to volunteer for it. It's a hard life, being the lump of grit that makes a pearl.'

'It must have been marvellous,' the publisher's publicity person said, opening her eyes very raptly, with a fascinated two fingers on her pointy chin.

'Poshlust, the desire to be posh, you know,' said Julie. 'I've got a huge display of Kelly's book, you know, in the middle of my window.'

'That's so, so marvellous,' the publisher's publicity person said.

Lorna herself was feeling awkward and unstylish. While she hadn't been looking, her sense of fashion had crept away. Her outfit had looked fine enough to her when she had checked it over at home, but now she was here, she could see it wasn't precise enough to offer the necessary protection. Waitresses brought round champagne and mini-sushi, and beautiful pink prawns, skewered on tiny toothpicks. Lorna was more used to cabbages these days, cabbages and turnips. Cabbages and turnips mashed up together with lots of pepper, and a dash of tomato ketchup, and a small slice of bargain-label blood sausage on the top.

Just then she saw Harriet, still tired-looking, still clad in her old brown velvet evening cloak. 'Dear comrade, I haven't seen you since poor Peter's funeral,' she said to Lorna, with a big kiss on each of Lorna's ever thinner white cheeks. 'Sorry I never rang you, I know I said I would. My dear, you know I'm pregnant – yes, again, I know. You'll come over for supper, of course, you will come, won't you. Come next week, but not on Monday or Tuesday . . .'

Lorna had long since stopped getting annoyed with Harriet and her dot dot dots. She couldn't help it, she was a caryatid, holding up that home of hers, the children, the husband, the stupid dog. Holding her prawn in front of her, she recalled the rusty taste of the sausage she had eaten with her lunch. It was the taste of the iron, possibly, that had set in on her soul.

Miranda had been filling in on Julie's job for a year now, and was finding it more difficult than anticipated to discern a suitable next move. She had taken on the once-adorable Daniel as her deputy, though he was well known to be barely literate and chronically disloyal. Something's not right here, Miranda thought to herself, nuzzling at her side-hair as she updated all her schedules; something is a burden. And so it was that Miranda languished onwards, correcting spelling mistakes in Daniel's headlines and gazing at his lovely profile, wondering who he was texting all day on his mobile, and what exactly it was that they were plotting against her.

But Lorna was thrilled to see Daniel at the launch party; he was still quite gorgeous, though something inside him was beginning to show round the chops. 'How are you doing?' she rushed over to say, all smiles. Daniel giggled in an embarrassed fashion and moved himself away.

'So how are you finding it these days, up there in that scary tower?' Lorna said to Annabel and Sidonie, Miranda's new juniors on the brainy-section desk. Miranda had briefed them thoroughly about Lorna, and anyway, Annabel remembered her well from that other party, when she had been really, really friendly and Lorna had been a nasty cat. 'Oh, it's cool, you know,' she said in her ironical Valley Girl accent. Sidonie flicked her hair and did her slow celebrity smile.

'Greetings, Lorna,' said Julie, sidling over, and shyly smiling. 'Greetings from the seaside, wish you were here and all that. Did you read the Kellster's tome then? Didn't she do well?'

Lorna hadn't, but she hoped to, shortly. She was waiting for the library on the precinct to get it in.

'It made me weep and sob like a little baby,' said Julie. 'Maybe I should be getting in on this memoir racket myself. I was a bullying victim myself, I think I told you, though I'd damn well nearly forgotten all about it. At middle school, a bunch of big girls, they picked on me something rotten. Then I damn near forgot all about it, until I read all that stuff in Kelly's book.'

'A bullying victim?' said Lorna, nicely. 'You mean a bully, surely? Or did that come later, as is so often the way?'

'They stripped me to my pants once,' said Julie, looking tearful. 'They stripped me to my pants once, they held me down in the mud. I was a victim first and foremost, Lorna. It does terrible things to you, having an experience like that.'

Lorna said: 'Yes, well.'

She held her pink prawn on its toothpick in front of her, she turned it round and round. It curled so helplessly under its darling organs, or would have done, if the darling organs hadn't been stripped out. We all want justification, is the problem, and it makes us all so very, very boring. She ran her finger round the rim of her glass, until it made its sweet high hum.

Lorna walked slowly across the parkland towards her tower, the grass trembling and glowing in the yellow sunlight of an early-autumn afternoon. A boy was shouting and pushing on a skate-board. A bunny danced across the football pitch, scut in air. The tall, slim-gridded structures floated above the park in a happy haze. She had in her pocket a note from Peter's widow: on his very deathbed, apparently, Peter had been begging her to return Lorna's book to her. 'I am sorry it has taken me so long to track you down, but I am sure you will understand. With thanks and all good wishes, Penny P.'

Every day on the scheme was a miracle, especially in warm and sunny weather. It was like a holiday park or a campus, purpose-built for the creation of happiness and well-being, unlikely and frankly foolish though the purpose had turned out to be. On days like this, though, you could feel the glory of the original intention, warm and sprightly in the air. You had to get closer to see the work of vandals and the cutting of maintenance budgets, year on year: the ground-floor child-size toilets, locked for good almost as soon as the buildings had opened; the balconies where the mothers were to smoke and hold their tea parties, stuck with satellite dishes and covered in chicken wire to keep the pigeons out.

They were militant modernists, the architects of these buildings; which is to say, though they would have denied it, they were great romantics at heart. They loved rigour, straight edges, difficult materials. They loved weather and rough nature, long treks through rainy clefts in mountains, unscalable sublimes. They had a horror of sentimentality and nostalgia, they had a horror of letting things slip back. They imagined a future that would not be like the past, but would instead be its total opposite: the opposite of slums, the opposite of darkness, the opposite of low and creeping and clinging to the ground. From privation they dreamt of plenty. From the middle of total wartime, they built a fantasy of peace.

They dreamt of tall buildings rising proudly, with no fear of engineering failure or night-time bombing raids. They dreamt of open spaces in the middle of cities, for the playing of rounders and netball, with no need to dig trenches in case of invasion, or allotments to plant their swedes and Brussels sprouts. They dreamt of people being able to live together happily, at high density, without cramping or regression; they dreamt of disposable consumer items without the growing heaps of fridges and bubble wrap and robbed bags. They dreamt of green parkland with children playing, no filthy nappies, no drugs, no nasty bullies. They dreamt of a world without rain in it, or pestilence, or daily dark.

'I hope you will all be good neighbours,' said Clement Attlee, the post-war Labour prime minister, opening the first block of new housing in 1945.

Lorna never had been back to the beautiful dry-cleaner: she had been about to take him that red-stained shirt, more than a year ago, when she changed her mind. She couldn't be bothered, she owed him nothing, or that was what she told herself. But she felt bad about it, and nervous, every time she walked past his door. She spotted Melanie and Joseph, making their slow, uncertain way along the path from the precinct towards the main door by the bins. She waved; Melanie and Joseph slowed yet further. It was nice of them to make the effort. It was nice of Lorna to make one back.

For Lorna, the revelation had come, really, sitting down and thinking about all that money she had in the building society. She mapped it out against the sums needed for even the smallest flat in London, now that house prices had risen steeply, now that she no longer had a job. Between her savings and her three-month pay-off, she could manage to support herself, supposing she spent little, for around a year. At the end of the year, she hoped, the way of things would be clearer. The privatisation of public housing had changed much, much more in the world about her than anything she and her ridiculous comrades had ever thought or done.

The radical bookshop had long since folded, for all sorts of business reasons, but not insignificant among them the way all its clever, bored young employees had been pilfering the books. Though by now more or less fully recovered from her brainstorm, Lorna still found herself confounded when she tried to remember which books from all her plunder she had actually read: gained under a cloud, under a cloud the books were to remain. Take, for example, Hegel's *Phenomenology*, even, that false springtime she spent on that book with Robin Moody, studying and annotating page by page. Had she read it before, or had she only dreamt it? Had she skimmed it, perhaps, in the greedy way of young scholars, and understood so little, it was as though she never did?

To clear the cloud, as a sort of penance, she started reading right through her book collection, taking notes on the books one by one. Once finished, she gave them to the library on the precinct. It would be the only local library in south London with collecting strengths in social theory and German idealism. That struck Lorna as a start. Things were less fun for Lorna, now that she had no nice clothes or any spare money, now that she no longer had a job. But she still had the city spread around her window, streets and streets of it in wheels and rows. Planes swooped, a helicopter thrashed across the lower currents. Energy bounced and sizzled from block to block.

Today, she was studying Rilke, in honour of poor Kelly, watching and noting on her computer the mighty looping movement of the *Duino Elegies*. The resting place, it seemed to her, comes not in the last poem, but in the next to last, the ninth, before the poet presses on, on, past death and his proper ending:

> ... *weil Hiersein viel ist, und weil uns scheinbar*
> *alles das Hiesige braucht, dieses Schwindende, das*
> *seltsam uns angeht. Uns, die Schwindendsten. Einmal*
> *jedes, nur einmal. Einmal und nichtmehr.*

> ... because being here is much, and because all this
> that's here, so fleeting, seems to require us and strangely
> concerns us. Us the most fleeting of all. Just once,
> everything, only for once. Once and no more.

'Oh, I'm writing my memoirs, you know,' she would say to people, on those odd occasions when she went out and ran into someone and they asked her what she was doing now. 'Oh, I'm writing my memoirs,' she would quip. She wasn't, though, she completely wasn't. All she did at her desk was study the works of other people; and most of those were dead.

'It simply isn't possible,' Lorna would say on the odd occasion she ran into someone she used to work with, 'to be a decent citizen when you're struggling to hold down a job of that sort. I had a brainstorm, did I ever tell you, it was like I just saw everything in front of me, mapped out.'

'I guess you have a point there,' the former colleague would say. As she did.

'That's why I decided to write my memoirs,' said Lorna, hitching her scruffy Scottish rucksack back on her shoulders, ready for the long trek home. The sky was deep blue and sizzling with ions. She'd be lucky to get halfway there, even, without getting completely soaked.

'So yes, I'm writing a sort of memoir,' said Lorna, as thunder crashed and the rain came spitting. Though actually, she was engaged on nothing of the sort.

Acknowledgements

Thanks to my family, Marion Turner, Edward Turner, Mark Robertson and Michael Turner, who lent me his Edinburgh flat. Thanks also to my friends, especially Carolyn Mills and Lynn Rose, and Becky Gardiner, Jean McNicol and David Thomson, who read and commented on early drafts. As, rigorously, did Georgia Garrett at A.P. Watt; thanks to her, and to her colleagues, Philippa Donovan and Naomi Leon. At Jonathan Cape, thanks to Dan Franklin, Alex Milner and Suzanne Dean. Thanks also to Steven Wells, who lent Julie a few of his choicest insults, and to Jason Cowley, who helped me trace my epigraph.

Special thanks to Mary Lynne Ellis, and most of all, to my beloved Matt Parton. This book is also for him, and for our son, Alexander.

The author is grateful for permission to reprint lines from the following:

Duino Elegies by Rainer Maria Rilke, translated by J. B. Leishman and Stephen Spender, published by Chatto & Windus. Reprinted by permission of The Random House Group. *Sonnets to Orpheus & Letters* by Rainer Maria Rilke, translated by Stephen Cohn, published by Carcanet Press Ltd, 2000. Reprinted by permission of Carcanet Press Ltd. *Phenomenology of Spirit* by G. W. F. Hegel, translated by A. V. Miller, published by Oxford University Press. Reprinted by permission of Oxford University Press. 'Lines On a Raised Beach' by Hugh MacDiarmid, taken from *The Hugh MacDiarmid Anthology*, edited by Grieve and Scott, published by Routledge, Keegan and Paul, 1972. Reprinted by permission of the Taylor & Francis Group. Lines from Steven Wells' NME articles © Steven Wells. Reprinted by permission of Steven Wells. 'Todesfuge' by Paul Celan, from *Mohn und Gedächtnis* © 1952 Deutsche Verlags-Anstalt, München, in der Verlagsgruppe Random House GmbH. *The Busconductor Hines* by James Kelman. © 1984 James Kelman. Reproduced by permission of the author c/o Rogers, Coleridge & White Ltd., 20 Powis Mews, London W11 1JN.

Every effort has been made to obtain necessary permissions with reference to copyright material. The publishers apologise if inadvertently any sources remain unacknowledged.